MAE MADDEN,

BY MARY MURDOCH MASON,

WITH AN

INTRODUCTORY POEM,

BY

JOAQUIN MILLER.

The wheel of fortune guide you,
The boy with the bow beside you
Run aye in the way, till the dawn of day
And a luckier lot betide you.
Ben Jonson.

CHICAGO:
JANSEN, McCLURG & CO.
1876.

FISH & KISSELL, PRINTERS.

A DREAM OF ITALY.

AN ALLEGORY INTRODUCING "MAE MADDEN."

I.

We two had been parted, God pity us, when
The stars were unnamed and when heaven was dim;
We two had been parted far back on the rim
And the outermost border of heaven's red bars:
We two had been parted ere the meeting of men
Or God had set compass on spaces as yet.
We two had been parted ere God had set
His finger to spinning the spaces with stars,—
And now, at the last in the gold and set
Of the sun of Venice, we two had met.

II.

Where the lion of Venice, with brows afrown,
With tossed mane tumbled, and teeth in air,
Looks out in his watch o'er the watery town,
With a paw half lifted, with his claws half bare,
By the blue Adriatic, in the edge of the sea,
I saw her. I knew her, but she knew not me.
I had found her at last! Why, I had sailed
The antipodes through, had sought, had hailed
All flags, had climbed where the storm clouds curled,
And called from the awful arched dome of the world.

III.

I saw her one moment, then fell back abashed
And filled full to the throat. . . . Then I turned me once more
So glad to the sea, while the level sun flashed
On the far, snowy Alps. . . . Her breast! Why, her breast
Was white as twin pillows that allure you to rest;
Her sloping limbs moved like to melodies, told
As she rose from the sea, and she threw back the gold
Of her glory of hair, and set face to the shore. . . .
I knew her! I knew her, though we had not met
Since the far stars sang to the sun's first set.

IV.

How long I had sought her! I had hungered, nor ate
Of any sweet fruits. I had tasted not one
Of all the fair glories grown under the sun.
I had sought only her. Yea, I knew that she
Had come upon earth and stood waiting for me
Somewhere by my way. But the pathways of fate
They had led otherwhere. The round world round,
The far North seas and the near profound
Had failed me for aye. Now I stood by that sea
While a ship drove by, and all dreamily.

V.

I had turned from the lion a time, and when
I looked tow'rd the tide and out on the lea
Of the town where the warm sea tumbled and teemed
With beauty, I saw her. I knew her then,
The tallest, the fairest fair daughter of men.

O, Venice stood full in her glory. She gleamed
In the splendor of sunset and sensuous sea;
Yet I saw but my bride, my affinity,
While the doves hurried home to the dome of Saint Mark
And the brass horses plunged their high manes in the dark.

VI.

Was it well with my love? Was she true? Was she brave
With virtue's own valor? Was she waiting for me?
O, how fared my love! Had she home? Had she bread?
Had she known but the touch of the warm-tempered wave?
Was she born upon earth with a crown on her head;
Or born like myself, but a dreamer, instead?
So long it had been! So long! Why the sea,
That wrinkled and surly old time-tempered slave,
Had been born, had his revels, grown wrinkled and hoar
Since I last saw my love on that uttermost shore.

VII.

O, how fared my love? Once I lifted my face
And I shook back my hair and looked out on the sea;
I pressed my hot palms as I stood in my place
And cried, "O, I come like a king to your side
Though all hell intervene." . . . "Hist! she may be a bride!
A mother at peace, with sweet babes on her knee!
A babe at her breast and a spouse at her side! . . .
Have I wandered too long, and has destiny
Set mortal between us?" I buried my face
In my hands, and I moaned as I stood in my place.

VIII.

'Twas her year to be young. She was tall, she was fair
Was she pure as the snow on the Alps over there?
'Twas her year to be young. She was fair, she was tall
And I knew she was true as I lifted my face
And saw her press down her rich robe to its place
With a hand white and small as a babe's with a doll.
And her feet—why, her feet, in the white shining sand,
Were so small they might nest in my one brawny hand.
Then she pushed back her hair with a round hand that shone
And flashed in the light with a white starry stone.

IX.

Then, my love she was rich. My love she was fair.
Was she pure as the snow on the Alps over there?
She was gorgeous with wealth. "Thank God, she has bread,"
I said to myself. Then I humbled my head
In gratitude. Then I questioned me where
Was her palace? her parents? What name did she bear?
What mortal on earth came nearest her heart?
Who touched the small hand till it thrilled to a smart?
'Twas her day to be young. She was proud, she was fair.
Was she pure as the snow on the Alps over there?

X.

Now she turned, reached a hand; then a tall gondolier
That had leaned on his oar, like a long lifted spear,
Shot sudden and swift and all silently
And drew to her side as she turned from the tide. . .
It was odd, such a thing, and I counted it queer

That a princess like this, whether virgin or bride,
Should abide thus apart, and should bathe in that sea;
And I shook back my hair, and so unsatisfied.
Then I fluttered the doves that were perched close about,
As I strode up and down in dismay and in doubt.

XI.

Then she stood in the boat on the borders of night
As a goddess might stand on that far wonder land
Of eternal sweet life, which men have named Death.
I turned to the sea and I caught at my breath,
As she drew from the boat through her white baby hand
Her vestment of purple imperial, and white.
Then the gondola shot! swift, sharp from the shore.
There was never the sound of a song or of oar
But the doves hurried home in white clouds to Saint
Mark,
And the lion loomed high o'er the sea in the dark.

XII.

Then I cried, "Quick! Follow her. Follow her.
Fast!
Come! Thrice double fare if you follow her true
To her own palace door." There was plashing of oar
And rattle of rowlock. . . . I sat leaning low
Looking far in the dark, looking out as we sped
With my soul all alert, bending down, leaning low.
But only the oaths of the men as we passed
When we jostled them sharp as we sudden shot thro'
The watery town. Then a deep, distant roar—
The rattle of rowlock, the rush of the oar.

XIII.

Then an oath. Then a prayer! Then a gust that made rents
Through the yellow sailed fishers. Then suddenly
Came sharp forked fire! Then far thunder fell
Like the great first gun! Ah, then there was route
Of ships like the breaking of regiments
And shouts as if hurled from an upper hell.
Then tempest! It lifted, it spun us about,
Then shot us ahead through the hills of the sea
As if a great arrow shot shoreward in wars—
Then heaven split open till we saw the blown stars.

XIV.

On! On! Through the foam, through the storm, through the town.
She was gone. She was lost in the wilderness
Of palaces lifting their marbles of snow.
I stood in my gondola. Up and all down
I pushed through the surge of the salt-flood street
Above me, below. . . Twas only the beat
Of thé sea's sad heart. . . Then I heard below
The water-rat building, but nothing but that;
Not even the sea bird screaming distress,
As she lost her way in that wilderness.

XV.

I listened all night. I caught at each sound;
I clutched and I caught as a man that drown'd. . . .
Only the sullen low growl of the sea
Far out the flood street at the edge of the ships.
Only the billow slow licking his lips,

Like a dog that lay crouching there watching for me;
Growling and showing white teeth all the night,
Reaching his neck and as ready to bite—
Only the waves with their salt flood tears
Fawning white stones of a thousand years.

XVI.

Only the birds in the wilderness
Of column and dome and of glittering spire
That thrust to heaven and held the fire
Of the thunder still: The bird's distress
As he struck his wings in that wilderness,
On marbles that speak and thrill and inspire. . .
The night below and the night above;
The water-rat building, the startled white dove,
The wide-winged, dolorous sea bird's call
The water-rat building, but that was all.

XVII.

Lo! pushing the darkness from pillar to post,
The morning came silent and gray like a ghost
Slow up the canal. I leaned from the prow
And listened. Not even the bird in distress
Screaming above through the wilderness;
Not even the stealthy old water-rat now.
Only the bell in the fisherman's tower
Slow tolling a-sea and telling the hour
To kneel to their sweet Santa Barbara
For tawny fishers a-sea and pray.

* * * * * *

XVIII.

My dream it is ended, the curtain withdrawn.
The night that lay hard on the breast of earth,
Deep and heavy as a horrid nightmare,
Moves by, and I look to the rosy dawn. . . . .
I shall leave you here, with a leader fair;
One gentle, with faith and fear of her worth.
She shall lead you on through that Italy
That the gods have loved; and may it be
A light-hearted hour that, hand in hand,
You wander the warm and the careless love-land.

XIX.

By the windy waters of the Michigan
She invokes the gods. . . . Be it bright or dim,
Who does his endeavor as best he can
Does bravely, indeed. The rest is with Him.
Let a new star dance in the Occident
Till it shakes through the gossamer floors of God
And shines o'er Chicago. . . The Orient
Is hoar with glories. Let Illini sod
Bear glory as well as the gleaming grain,
And engines smoking along her plain.

JOAQUIN MILLER.

CHICAGO, Nov., 1875.

MAE MADDEN.

CHAPTER I.

SCENE. Deck of an ocean steamer.

Characters. Mrs. Jerrold, matron and chaperon in general.

Edith Jerrold, her daughter.

Albert Madden, a young man on study intent.

Eric, his brother, on pleasure bent.

Norman Mann, cousin of the Jerrolds, old classmate of the Maddens.

Mae Madden, sister of the brothers and leading lady.

T'S something like dying, I do declare," said Mae, and as she spoke a suspicious-looking drop slid softly across her cheek, down over the deck-railing, to join its original briny fellows in the deep below.

"What is like dying?" asked Eric.

"Why, leaving the only world you know. There, you see, papa and mamma are fast fading away, and here we are traveling off at the rate of ever so many miles an hour."

"Knots, Mae; do be nautical at sea."

"Away from everything and everybody we know. I do really think it is like dying,—don't you, Mr. Mann?" Mae turned abruptly and faced the young man by her side.

"People aren't apt to die in batches or by the half-dozen," he replied, coolly. "If you were all by yourself, it would be more like it, I suppose, but you are taking quite a slice of your own world along with you, and really—"

"And really pity is the very last article I have any use for. You are right. I was only sorry for the moment. 'Eastward Ho' is a very happy cry. How differently we shall all take Europe," she continued, in a moment. "There is Albert, I honestly believe he will live in his Baedeker just because he can see no further than the covers of a book. You need not laugh, for it is a fact that people confined for years to a room can't see beyond its limits when they are taken out into broader space, and I don't see why it shouldn't be the same with a man who lives in his books as Albert does."

"He sees the world in his books," said Mr. Mann, with a little spirit.

"He gets a microscopic view of it, yes," replied Mae, grandiloquently, "and Edith—"

"Always sees just what he does," suggested Eric maliciously.

"Now, boys," said Miss Mae, assuming suddenly a mighty patronage, "I will not have you hit at Albert and Edith in this way. It will be very annoying to them. They have a right to act just as absurdly as they choose. We none of us know how people who are falling in love would act."

No, the boys agreed this was quite true.

"And I really do suppose they are falling in love, don't you?" queried Mae.

Yes, they did both believe it.

Just here, up came the two subjects of conversation, looking, it must be confessed, as much like one subject as any man and wife.

"What are you talking of?" asked Edith, "Madame Tussaud or a French salad? No matter how trivial the topic, I am sure it has a foreign flavor."

"There you are mistaken," replied the frank Eric, "we were discussing you two people, in the most homelike kind of a way."

At this Edith blushed, Albert frowned, Mae scowled at Eric, who opened his eyes amazedly, Norman Mann looked over the deck railing and laughed, the wind blew, the sailors heave-ho-ed near by, and there was a grand tableau vivant for a few seconds.

"O, come," cried Mae, "suppose we stop looking like a set of illustrations for a phrenological journal, expressive of the various emotions. I was only speculating on the different sights we should see in the same places. Confess, now, Albert. Won't your eyes be forever hunting out old musty, dusty volumes? Will not books be your first pleasures in the sight-seeing line?"

"O, no, pictures," cried Edith.

"That is as you say," Mae demurely agreed. "Pictures and books for you two at any rate."

"And churches."

"For your mother, yes, and beer-gardens for Eric, and amphitheatres and battle fields for Mr. Mann."

"And for yourself?"

"The blue, blue bay of Naples, a grove of oranges, moonlight and a boat if it please you."

"By the way," suggested Albert, "about our plans; we really should begin to agitate the matter at once."

"Yes, to do our fighting on shipboard. Let us agree to hoist the white flag the day we sight land, else we shall settle down into a regular War of the Roses and never decide," laughed Norman.

"As there are six minds," continued Albert, "there will have to be some giving up."

"Why do you look at me?" enquired Mae. "I am the very most unselfish person in the world. I'll settle down anywhere for the winter, provided only that it is not in Rome."

"But that is the very place," cried Edith, and Albert, and Mrs. Jerrold from her camp-chair.

"O, how dreadful! The only way to prevent it will be for us to stand firm, boys, and make it a tie."

"But Norman is especially eager to go to Rome," said Edith, "and that makes us four strong at once in favor of that city."

"But is not Rome a fearful mixture of dead Cæsar's bones and dirty beggars? And mustn't one carry hundreds of dates at one's finger-tips to appreciate this, and that, and the other? Is it not all tremendously and overwhelmingly historical, and don't you have to keep exerting your mind and thinking and remembering? I would rather go down to Southern Italy and look at lazzaroni lie on stone walls, in red cloaks, as they do in pictures, and not be obliged to topple off the common Italian to pile the gray stone with old memories of some great dead man. Everything is ghostly in

Rome. Now, there must be some excitement in Southern Italy. There's Vesuvius, and she isn't dead—like Nero—but a living demon, that may erupt any night, and give you a little red grave by the sea for your share."

"She's not nearly through yet," laughed Edith, as Mae paused for breath.

"I'm only afraid," said Mae, "that after I had been down there a week, I should forget English, buy a contadina costume, marry a child of the sun, and run away from this big world with its puzzles and lessons, and rights and wrongs. Imagine me in my doorway as you passed in your travelling carriage, hot and tired on your way—say to Sorrento. I would dress my beautiful Italian all up in scarlet flowers and wreathe his big hat and kiss his brown eyes and take his brown hand, and then we would run along by the bay and laugh at you stiff, grand world's folks as we skipped past you."

"We shall know where to look for you, if ever you do disappear," said Norman Mann.

"But, my dear Mae," added Albert, "though this is amusing, it is utterly useless."

"Amusing things always are," said Mae.

"The question is, shall we or shall we not go to Rome for the winter?"

"Certainly, by all means, and if I don't like it, I'll run away to Sorrento," and Mae shook her sunny head and twinkled her eyes in a fascinating sort of way, that made Eric feel a proud brotherly pleasure in this saucy young woman, and that gave Norman Mann a sort of feeling he had had a good deal of late, a feeling hard to define, though we have all known it, a delicious concoction of pleasure and pain. His eyes were fixed on Mae, now. "What is it?" she asked. "You will like Rome, I am sure." "No, I never like what I think I shall not."

"It might save some trouble, then, if I ask you now if you expect to like me," said he, in a lower tone. "Why certainly, I do like you very much," she replied, honestly. "What a stupid question," he thinks, vexedly. "Why did I tell him I liked him?" she thinks, blushingly. So the waves of anxiety and doubt begin to swell in these two hearts as the outside waves beat with a truer sea-motion momently against the steamer's side.

Between days of sea-sickness come delightful intervals of calm sea and fresh breezes, when the party fly to the hurricane deck to get the very quintessence of life on the ocean wave. One morning Mrs. Jerrold and Edith were sitting there alone, with rugs and all sorts of head devices in soft wools and flannels, and books and a basket of fruit. The matron of the party was a tall, fine-looking woman, a good type of genuine New England stock softened by city breeding. New Englanders are so many propositions from Euclid, full of right angles and straight lines, but easy living and the dressmaker's art combine to turn the corners gently. Edith was like her mother, but softened by a touch of warm Dutch blood. She was tall, almost stately, with a good deal of American style, which at that time happened to be straight and slender. She was naturally reserved, but four years of boarding-school life had enriched her store of adjectives and her amount of endearing gush-power, and she had at least six girl friends to whom she sent weekly epistles of some half-dozen sheets in length, beginning, each one of them, with "My dearest——" and ending "Your devoted Edith."

As Edith and her mother quietly read, and ate grapes, and lolled in a delightfully feminine way, voices were heard,—Mae's and Norman's. They were in the middle of a conversation. "Yes," Mae was saying, "you do away with individuality altogether nowadays, with your dreadful classifications. It is all the same from daffodils up to women."

"How do we classify women, pray?"

"In the mind of man," began Mae, as if she were reading, "there are three classes of women; the giddy butterflies, the busy bees, and the woman's righters. The first are pretty and silly; the second, plain and useful; the third, mannish and odious. The first wear long trailing dresses and smile at you while waltzing, the second wear aprons and give you apple-dumplings, and the third want your manly prerogatives, your dress-coat, your money, and your vote. Flirt with the giddy butterflies, your first love was one. First loves always are. Marry the busy bee. Your mother was a busy bee. Mothers always are. And keep on the other side of the street from the woman's righter as long as you can. Alas! your daughter will be one."

"Well, isn't there any classifying on the other side? Aren't there horsemen and sporting men and booky men, in the feminine mind?"

"Perhaps so. There certainly are the fops, and nowadays this terrible army of reformers and radicals, of whom my brother Albert here is the best known example."

"What is it?" asked Albert, looking up abstractedly from his book, for he and Eric had sauntered up the stairs too, by this time.

"They are the creatures," continued Mae, "who scorn joys and idle pleasures. They deal with the good of the many and the problems of the universe, and step solemnly along to that dirge known as the March of Progress. And what do they get for it all? Something like this. Put down your book, I'm going to prophesy," and Mae backed resolutely up against the railing and held her floating scarfs and veils in a bunch at her throat, while she prophesied in this way:

"Behold me, direct lineal descendant of Albert Madden, speaking to my children in the year 1995: 'What, children, want amusement? Want to see the magic lantern to note the effects of light? Alas! how frivolous. Listen, children, to the achievements of your great ancestor, as reported by the Encyclopedia. "A. Madden—promoter of civilization and progress, chiefly known by his excellent theory entitled The Number of Cells in a Human Brain compared to the Working Powers of Man, and that remarkable essay, headed by this formula: Given—10,000,000 laboring men, to find the number of loaves of bread in the world." Here, children, take these works. Progressimus, you may have the theory, while Civilizationica reads the essay. Then change about. Ponder them well, and while we walk to the Museum later, tell me their errors. Then I will show you the preserved ears of the first man found in Boshland by P. T. Barnum, jr.' Oh, bosh," said Mae suddenly, letting fly her streamers, "what a dry set of locusts you nineteenth century leaders are. You are devouring our green land, and some of us butterflies would like to turn our yellow wings into solid shields against you, if we could. There, I've made a goose of myself again on the old subject. Edith, there's the lunch bell. Take me down before I say another word." Exeunt feminines all.

"Where did the child pick up all that?" queried Albert.

"'All that' is in the air just now," answered Norman. "It is a natural reaction of a strong physical nature against the utilitarian views of the day. Miss Mae is a type of—"

"O, nonsense, what prigs you are," interrupted Eric, "Mae is jolly. Do stop your reasoning about her. If you are bound to be a potato yourself to help save the masses from starvation, don't grumble because she grew a flower. Come, let us go to lunch too."

Conversation was not always of this sort. One evening, not long after, there was a moon, and Edith and Albert were missing. Eric was following a blue-eyed girl along the deck, and Mae and Norman wandered off by themselves up to this same hurricane deck again. The moonlight was wonderful. It touched little groups here and there and fell full on the face of a woman in the steerage, who sat with her arms crossed on her knee and her face set eastward. She was singing, and her voice rose clearly above the puff of the engine and the jabber below. There was a chorus to the song, in which rough men and tired looking women joined. The song was about home, and once in a while the girl unclasped her arms and passed her hands over her eyes. Mae and Norman Mann looked at her silently. "I suppose we don't know when we make pictures," said Mae. "Don't we?" asked Norman pointedly. Mae looked very reprovingly out from her white wraps at him, but he smiled back composedly and admiringly, and drew her hand a trifle closer in his arm. And saucy Mae began to feel in that sort of purring mood women come to when they drop the bristling, ready-for-fight air with which they start on an acquaintance. Perhaps, if the steamer had been a sailing-vessel, there would have been no story to tell about Mae Madden, for a long line of evenings, and girls singing songs, and hurricane decks by moonlight, are dangerous things. But the vessel was a fast steamer, and was swiftly nearing land again.

CHAPTER II.

ROME, February, 18—.

MY DEAR MAMMA: — Yes, it is Rome, mamma, and everybody is impressed. The boys talk of emperors all the time; Edith is wild over Madonnas and saints, and Mrs. Jerrold runs from Paul's house to Paul's walks and Paul's drives and Paul's stand at the prisoner's bar, and reads the Acts through five times a day, in the most religious and Romanistic spirit. No one could make more fuss over a patron saint, I am sure. For my part, I feel as if I were in the most terrible ghost story. The old Romans are all around me. Underneath the street noises, I seem to hear cries, and in the air I half see a constant flashing of swords and scars and blood, and I can't even put my foot on the Roman pavement without wondering which dead Cæsar my saucy Burt boot No. 2 is walking over. I shouldn't mind trampling old Caligula, but I don't like the thought on general principles. I feel all out of place, so modern and fixed up and flimsy. If I could get into old picturesque clothes and out of the English-speaking quarter, I should not be so oppressed and might worship Rome. But I seriously think I shall die if I stay here much longer. There's a spirit-malaria that eats into my life. I feel as if all the volumes of Roman history bound in heavy vellum, that papa has in his study, were laid right on top of my little heart, so that every time it beats, it thumps against them, and I assure you, mamma, its worse than dyspepsia. If I could only get out on a New England hillside, where there were no graves more important than those of grasshoppers and butterflies! What should I do when I got there? Take off my hat, and scream for joy, and feel free and glad to be in a fresh country, with rich, warm, untainted earth and young life.

But all this is nonsense, mamma, and I shouldn't be writing it, if I hadn't just come from the catacombs of St. Calixtus. To think of Albert's insisting upon going there the very first thing! But so he did, and so we went, and talked solemnly about the Appian Way, and saw everybody's tombs and ashes, and quoted poetry, until I stuck a pin in Albert's arm and sang Yankee Doodle, to keep from crying. Then, oh, how shocked they looked. Even Mr. Mann seemed ashamed of me. When we reached the place, we each took a candle and the guide led the way down into the bowels of the earth. Mamma, they are very unpleasant. There were two German youths along, and green lizards crawled all over. They winked at me. The way grew so narrow that we had to walk one by one through lines of wall perforated with holes for dead bodies. Once in a while we would come to a small chapel, for miserable variety's sake, and be told to admire some very old, very wretched painting. Jonah and the whale were represented in a double-barreled miracle picture. Not only was the whale about to swallow Jonah, but he was only as large as a good-sized brook trout, while Jonah towered away above him like a Goliath. I found myself wondering if the guide had convulsions, and if he should have one now, and die, how many days would pass before we should eat each other. And would they take me first, because I am youngest and plumpest? Albert would make good soup bones, and Eric's shoulder serve as a delicious fore-quarter. And by the time we came to the top again, I was all ready to cry. And then, mamma, I did an awful thing. Mr. Mann exclaimed: "Why, Miss Mae, how frightened you look. You are quite white." And I answered very sharply: "What a disagreeable man you are. I'm not frightened at all." I said it in a dreadful tone, and how his face changed. He looked so strangely. Everybody was still but Albert, and he said, "Why, Mae, you are very rude to Mr. Mann." Even then I didn't apologize. So here we are at sword's points, and all the rest sympathizing with my foe, who is only on the defensive. Why am I such a belligerent? I can't conceive where I got my nature, unless from that very disagreeable dear old grandpapa of papa's, who fought the whole world all his life. But how egotistic I am, even to my mother. Of course you want to know how we are lodged and clothed and fed. We have taken apartments, as I presume Albert wrote you, on the Via San Nicolo da Tolentino, quite near the Costanzi hotel, which is in the heigth of the fashion as a hotel; near too, which is better, to Mr. Story's studio and the old Barberini palace and the Barberini square and fountains. Off behind, is that terrible church of the Cappucini, with its cemetery underneath of bones and skulls and such horrors. I like the apartments very much, principally because I have made three staunch friends and one good enemy, in the kitchen. The *padrona*,—she's the woman who keeps the house, and serves us, too, in this case—though Mrs. Jerrold has a maid to wait on the table and care for our rooms—well, the *padrona* is my first friend. Her cousin, a handsome southern Italian, is here on a visit, and she is not only my friend, but my instructress. She tells me lovely stories about her home and the peasants and their life, while I sit on the floor with Giovanni,—friend number three and eldest son of the padrona,—and even Roberto, my enemy, the crying baby of three years, hushes his naughty mouth to listen to Lisetta, for that is the cousin's name. I am so glad I studied Italian as hard as I did for my music, for it comes very easily to me now, and already I slip the pretty words from my halting tongue much more smoothly and quickly than you would imagine I could. Mrs. Jerrold isn't quite satisfied, and would prefer the Costanzi, only she doesn't believe in letting us girls stay at large hotels. She and Edith are shocked at my kitchen tastes, so that I generally creep off quietly and say nothing about it. It is strange for me to have to keep anything secret, but I am learning how.

As for our clothes, O, mamma, Edith is ravishing in a deep blue-black silk, with a curly, wavy sort of fringe on it, and odd loopings here and there where you don't expect to find them. What can't a Parisian dressmaker do? They have such a wonderful idea of appropriateness, it seems to me. Now, at home you know we girls always wear the same sort of thing, but Madame H—— says no, Edith, and I should dress very differently; and now Edith's clothes all have a flow, and sweep, and grace about them, and her silks rustle in a stately way as she walks, while my dresses haven't any trimming to speak of, but are cut in a clinging, square sort of way, with jackets, and here and there a buckle, that makes me feel half the time as if I were playing soldier in a lady-like fashion. But what a budget this is. How shocked the people here would be. They take travel so solemnly, mamma, and treat Baedeker, like the Bible,—and here am I crushing down Rome, and raising Paris on top of it. Indeed, I can't help it, for Paris is utterly intoxicating. It takes away your moral nature and adds it all into your powers of enjoyment. Well, good-bye, my dear, and keep writing me tremendous letters, won't you; for I do love you dearly.

Your loving daughter,

MAE.

Mae felt a great deal better when she had finished the letter, and, like a volatile girl as she was, buttoned her Burt boots and Paris gloves, singing gaily a dash from Trovatore in a very light-hearted manner.

"Why, you look like a different girl," cried Eric, as she entered the parlor, where he and Mr. Mann were sitting. "Mrs. Jerrold, Edith, and Albert have gone on in a carriage, and you are left to my tender care; will you ride or walk?"

"How can you ask? My feet are quite wild. No wonder I am a different girl. Are we not going to the Pincian hill to look at the live world and people? I have just unlocked the stop-gates and let the blood bound in my veins as it wants to."

"It has been taking the *cinque-pace,* I should say from your long face to-day."

"O, it has only been trying to keep step with the march of the ages, or some such stately tread, but it was hard work, and now the dear life of me hops, skips and jumps, like this," and Mae seized her brother and danced across the room, stopping very near Mr. Mann, who stood with his back to them, drumming on the window pane. She looked at him quizzically and half raised her eyebrows.

Eric shook his head, and said aloud in his outspoken way: "You owe him an apology, Mae, for this morning's rudeness."

Mr. Mann turned quickly. "I am surprised, Eric. Let your sister find out for herself when she is rude."

"Bless me," cried Eric, "what is the row?"

Mae looked determined. "Are you going to the Pincian with us?" she asked.

"No, I am going to stay home."

"Well, good-bye, then. Come, Eric." The door closed behind them.

Mr. Mann stood by the window and watched them walk away. Mae, with her eager, restless, fresh life showing out in every motion; Eric, with his boy-man air and his student swing and happy-go-lucky toss of his head. Mr. Mann smiled and then he sighed. "That's a good boy, so square and fair and merry—and a queer girl," he added. "Rome isn't the place for her. She must get away, though why I should take care for her, or worry about her, little vixen, I don't see." Still he smiled as one would over a very winning, very wicked child, and shortly after took his hat and went to the Pincio, after all.

Meantime, the brother and sister had walked gaily along, passed the Spanish Steps, and were on the Pincian hill. Here, Mae was indeed happy. The fine equipages and dark, rich beauty of the Italians delighted her, and she and Eric found a shaded bench, and watched the carriages drive round and round, and criticised, and admired, and laughed like two idle children. They bought some flowers, and Mae sat pulling them to pieces, when they caught sight, down the pathway, of two approaching Piedmontese officers.

"O," cried Mae, and dropped her flowers, and clasped her hands, and sprang to her feet, "O, Eric, are they gods or men?"

The Piedmontese officer is godlike. He must be of a certain imposing height to obtain his position, and his luxurious yellow moustaches and blue black eyes, enriched and intensified by southern blood, give him a strange fascination. The cold, manly beauty and strength of a northern blonde meet with the heat and lithe grace of the more supple southerner to produce this paragon. There is a combination of half-indolent elegance and sensuous langour, with a fire, a verve, a nobility, that puts him at the very head of masculine beauty. Add to the charms of his physique, the jauntiest, most bewitching of uniforms, the clinking spurs, the shining buttons, the jacket following every line of his figure, and no wonder maidens' hearts seek him out always and young pulses beat quicker at his approach.

Mae's admiration was simply rapturous. Utterly regardless of the pretty picture she herself made, of her vivid coloring and sparkling beauty, she stood among her dropped flowers until the two pairs of eyes were fixed upon her. Then she became suddenly aware of her attitude and with quick feminine cunning endeavored to transfer her admiration to some beautiful horses cantering by, exclaiming in Italian, that the officers might surely understand she was thinking only of the fine animals: " O, what wonderful horses!"

The foreign pronunciation, Eric's amusement, Mae's confusion, were not lost upon the men. Their curiosity was piqued, their eyes and pride gratified. They sauntered leisurely past, only to turn a corner and quicken their steps again toward the bench where Eric and Mae were seated. They found the brother and sister just arising, and followed them slowly.

An Italian is quick to detect secrets. The two had not proceeded far before one said to the other: "Eh, Luigi, we are not the only interested party."

Luigi looked slowly around and saw a crowd of Italian loungers gazing at the little stranger with their softly-bold black eyes full of admiration. He shrugged his shoulders slightly. "Bah, they gaze in that way at all womankind. See, now they are watching the next one," and as he spoke, the boys turned with one accord to stare at a young Italian girl, who pressed closer to the side of her hook-nosed old duenna.

"It is not those loungers that I noticed," replied the other. "Look there," and he waved his hand lightly toward the left, where, under a large-leafed tree, gazing apparently in idleness, stood a young man.

"Ah," said Luigi, still incredulous, "he sees nothing but Rome; he is fresh from over the seas."

"No, no, watch his eyes," replied the other.

They were assuredly fixed, with a keen searching glance, on a little form before them, and as Eric and Mae suddenly turned to the left, the stranger, half carelessly, but very quickly, crossed to another path, from which he could watch them, but be, in his turn, unobserved.

"Jealous," laughed Luigi, shrugging his shoulders again. "Her lover, probably."

"No," replied Bero, "but he may be some time." Then after a moment's pause, "Good evening," he said carelessly. "I am going to say my prayers at vespers. I've been a sorry scamp of late."

Luigi laughed disdainfully and lightly. "You want to get rid of me? Well, be it so. I don't want to lose my heart over a little foreigner. I have other game. However, Lillia shall not know of it. Addio, Bero." So Luigi went off the other way, and Bero, with a flushed face, followed Mae at a distance, and kept an eye on the stranger, flattering himself that he was quite unnoticed by those sharp, keen eyes. He was mistaken. Norman Mann had seen the officers before they saw him, had watched their footsteps, and had a pretty clear idea of the whole affair.

Mae walked on happily, chatting with Eric,

and with that vague, delightful feeling of something exciting in the air. She knew there was an officer behind her, because she had heard the clicking spurs, but she only guessed that he might be one of the two who had passed—the taller, perhaps,—which, of course, he was. She had, moreover, in some mysterious way, caught sight of a figure resembling Norman Mann, trying, she thought, to avoid her. Her spirits rose with the half-mystery, and she grew brighter and prettier and more magnetic to the two followers as she tossed her shoulders slightly and now and then half-turned her sunny head.

As for Eric, he was totally unconscious of any secrets. He fancied himself and his pretty, nice, little sister all alone by their very selves, and he went so far as to expatiate on the vastness of the world, and how in this crowd there was no other life that bordered or touched on theirs.

To which Mae replied : "You don't know; you may fall in love with one of these very Italian girls, or my future husband may be walking behind me now." When she had said this, she flushed scarlet and was very much ashamed of herself in her heart.

"We must go home now," Eric replied, quite disdaining such sybilistic remarks. So they left the hill and went down the Steps in the rich afternoon light, and so homewards. Of course the Italian and Mr. Mann still followed them ; Norman on the other side of the street, the Italian in a slyer, less conspicuous manner, by taking side streets, or the next parallel pavement, and appearing only at every corner in the distance. He appeared, however, close at hand, as Mae and Eric turned into their lodgings. His eyes met Mae's. She blushed involuntarily as she recognized him, and at once, in that moment, there was an invisible half-acquaintance established between the two. If they should ever meet again, they would remember each other.

Mae crept off to the kitchen that evening, to beg for another of Lisetta's stories, and quite forgot her walk, the officer, and Norman Mann while she listened to the

STORY OF TALILA.

Talila was a young girl, destined to be a nun. She was a naughty little girl and would make wry faces at the thought, and wish she could be a man, a soldier or a sailor, instead of being a woman and a nun ; and as she grew older she would dance all the time, and didn't say her prayers very much, and was so bad that the priest sent for her to see him. He told her how wicked she was, and that, too, when she was to be the bride of the church ; but she said the church had many, many brides, and she would rather be the bride of Giovanni ; and that she loved red-cheeked babies better than beads, and songs were nicer than prayers. Should she sing him such a pretty, gay one she knew? And the priest could hardly keep from laughing at the bright-eyed, naughty, naughty Talila. But he said : "If Giovanni does not want to marry you, will you then become the bride of the church ?" And Talila laughed aloud and tossed her head. "Giovanni longs to marry me, Father," she said, "I know that already." But the Father sent for Giovanni and gave him money if he would say he did not want to marry Talila. At first he would not say so, but the Father showed him a purse all full of silver, which Talila's mother had brought him, for it was she who had vowed Talila should be a nun. Then the Father said : "This is yours if you say as I wish, and if not, you shall be cursed forever, and all your children shall be cursed, because you have married the bride of the church." Then Giovanni crossed himself and took the bag of silver, and the priest sent for Talila, and she heard her Giovanni say he didn't want to marry her—she had better be a nun; and she threw up her brown arms and screamed aloud, and fell down as if dead. And afterwards she was very ill, and when she grew better she had forgotten everything and was only a little child, and she loves little children, and is ever with them, but she calls them all Giovanni. They play together by the bay through the long day, and at night she takes them to their mothers, and goes alone to her home. But alas! she never tells her beads, or prays a prayer, and sorry things are said of her—that God gave her up because she left Him. But the children all love her, and she loves them.

CHAPTER III.

EDITH and Mae had a quarrel one morning. Mae's tongue was sharp, but although she breezed quickly, she calmed again very soon. The latter fact availed her little this time, for Edith maintained a cold displeasure that would not be melted by any bright speeches or frank apologies. "Edith," said little Miss Mae, quite humbly for her, as she put on her hat, and drew on her gloves, "Edith, aren't you going out with me?" "What for?" asked that young person indifferently.

"Why—for fun, and to make up. Haven't you forgiven me yet?"

Edith did not reply directly. "I am going out with mamma to buy our dominoes for the Carnival, and to see our balcony. Albert has engaged one for us, on the corner of the Corso and Santa Maria e Jesu. I suppose you can go too. There will be an extra seat. We'll come home by the Pincian Hill."

"Thank you," said Mae, "but I will get Eric and go for a tramp," and she left the room with compressed lips and flushed cheeks. In the hall were Albert, Eric and Norman, talking busily. "Where are you going Eric, mayn't I go too, please?" "I'm sorry Mae, but this is an entirely masculine affair—five-button gloves and parasols are out of the question."

"O, Ric, I am half lonely." Mae laughed a little hysterically. At that moment she caught Mr. Mann's eyes, full of sympathy. "But good-bye," she added, and opened the door, "I'm going."

"Alone?" asked Norman, involuntarily.

"Yes, alone," replied Mae. "Have you any objections, boys?" Eric and Albert were talking busily and did not hear her. Norman Mann held open the door for her to pass out, and smiled as she thanked him. She smiled back. She came very near saying, "I'm sorry I was rude the other day, forgive me," and he came very near saying, "May I go with you, Miss Mae?" But they neither of them spoke, and Norman closed the door with a sigh, and Mae walked away with a sigh. It was only a little morning's experience, sharp words, misunderstandings; but the child was young, far from home and her mother, and it seemed hard to her. She was in a very wild mood, a very hard mood, and yet all ready to be softened by a kind, sympathetic word, so nearly do extremes of emotion meet.

"There's no one to care a pin about me," said she to herself, "not a pin. I have a great mind to go and take the veil or drown myself in the Tiber. Then they would be bound to search for me, and convent vows and Tiber mud hold one fast. No, I won't, I'll go and sit in the Pincian gardens and talk Italian with the very first person I meet and forget all about myself. I wish Mr. Mann wouldn't pity me. Dear me, here I am remembering these forlorn people again. I wish I could see mamma and home this morning,—the dear old library. Why the house is shut up and mamma's south. I forgot that, and here am I all alone. It is like being dead. There, I have dropped a tear on my tie and spoiled it! Besides, if one is dead, there comes Heaven. Why shouldn't I play dead, and make my own Heaven?" Here Mae seated herself, for she was on the Pincio by this time, and looked off at the view, at that wonderful view of St. Peter's, the Tiber, all the domes and rising ruins and afar the campagna. "I wouldn't make my Heaven here," thought this dreadful Mae, "not if it is beautiful. I'd not stay here a single other day. Bah no!" and she shook her irreverent little fist right down at the Eternal City.

At this moment, a small beggar, who had been pleading unnoticed at her side, was lifted from his feet by a powerful hand, and a shower of soft Italian imprecations fell on Mae's ear. She sprang up quickly, "No, no," she cried in Italian, "how dare you hurt a harmless boy?" She lifted her face full toward that of the man who had inspired her wrath, and her eyes met those of the Piedmontese officer. She blushed scarlet.

"Pardon, a thousand pardons," began he. "It was for your sake, Signorina. I saw you shake your hand that he should leave you, and I fancied that the little scamp was troubling the foreign lady."

Mae laughed frankly, although she was greatly confused. The officer and the beggar boy behind him waited expectantly. "I shook my hand at my thoughts," she explained. "I did not see the boy. Forgive me, Signor, for my hasty words."

The officer enjoyed her confusion quietly. He threw a handful of small coin at the beggar, and bade him go. Then he turned again to

Mae. "I am sorry, Signorina, that your thoughts are sad. I should think they would all be like sweet smiles." He said this with an indescribable delicacy and gallantry, as if he half feared to speak to her, but his sympathy must needs express itself.

Mae was, as we have seen, in a reckless, wild mood. She did not realize what she was doing. She had just broken down all barriers in her mind, was dead to her old life, and ready to plan for Heaven. And here before her stood a wonderful, sympathizing, new friend, who spoke in a strange tongue, lived in a strange land, was as far removed from her old-time people and society as an inhabitant of Saturn, or an angel. She accepted him under her excitement, as she would have accepted them. No waiting for an introduction, no formal getting-acquainted talk, no reserve. She looked into the devoted, interested eyes above her, and said frankly:

"I was feeling all alone, and I hate Rome. I thought I would like to play I was dead, and plan out a Heaven for myself. It should not be in Rome. And then I suppose I shook my fist."

"Where would your Heaven be?" asked the Piedmontese, falling quickly, with ready southern sympathy, into her mood. Mae seated herself on the bench and made room for him at her side.

"Where should it be?" she repeated. "Down among the children of the sun, all out in the rich orange fields, by the blue Bay of Naples, I think, with Vesuvius near by, and Capri; yes, it would be in Sorrento that I should find my heaven."

The officer smiled under his long moustaches. "For three days,—at a hotel, Signorina."

"No, no; with the peasants. I am tired and sick of books, and people, and reasons. Shall I give you a day of my Heaven?"

Bero smiled and bent slightly forward and rested his hand lightly on the stick of her parasol, which lay between them. "Go on," he said.

"I would fill my apron with sweet flowers and golden fruit—great oranges, and those fragrant, delicious tiny mandarins—and I would get a crowd of little Italians about me, all a-babbling their pretty, pretty tongue, and I would go down to the bay and get in an anchored boat, and lie there all the morning, catching the sunlight in my eyes, trimming the brown babies and the boat with flowers, looking off at the water and the clouds, tossing the pretty fruit, and laughing, and playing, and enjoying. Later, there'd be a run on the beach, and a ride on a donkey, and a dance, with delirious music and frolic. And then the moon and quiet,—and I would steal away from the crowd, and take a little boat, and float and drift—"

"Alone?" asked Bero, softly. "Surely, you wouldn't condemn a mountaineer's yellow moustache, or a soldier's spurs and sword, if at heart he was really a child of the sun also? May I share your day of Heaven? It would be paradise for me, too." All this in the same soft, deferential manner.

"Well, well," half laughed, half sighed Mae. "All this is a dream, unless, indeed, I go home with Lisetta."

"Who is Lisetta?"

"Our *padrona's* cousin. She is here on a visit. She lives within a mile of Sorrento, on the coast. She goes home at the end of Carnival. Oh, how I do long for Carnival," continued Mae, frankly and confidentially. "Don't you? I am like a child over it. I am trying already to persuade Eric—that is my brother—to take me down on the Corso the last night, for the Mocoletti. It would be much better fun than staying on our balcony."

"Where is your balcony?" asked Bero, stroking his long moustaches.

"It is on the corner of Maria e Jesu, and if I ever see you coming by, I shall be tempted to pepper your pretty uniform. How beautiful it is!"

"Yes," replied Bero, again gazing proudly down at his lithe figure, in its well-fitting clothes, "but I would be willing to be showered with confetti daily to see you. How shall I know you? What is to be the color of your domino?" And he bent forward, hitting his spurs against the paving stones, flashing his deep eyes, and half reaching out his hand, in that same tender, respectful way.

Mae saw the sunlight strike his hair; she half heard his deep breath; and, like a flood, there suddenly swept over her the knowledge that this new friend, this sympathizing soul, was an unknown man, and that she was a girl. What had she done? What could she do? Confusion and embarrassment suddenly overtook her. She bent her eyes away from those other eyes, that were growing bolder and more tender in their gaze. "I—I—" she began, and just at this very inauspicious moment, while she sat there, flushed, by the stranger's side, the clatter of swiftly-approaching wheels sounded, and a carriage turned the corner, containing Mrs. Jerrold, Edith, Albert, and Norman Mann. They all saw her.

Mae laughed. It was such a dreadful situation that it was funny, and she laughed again. "Those are my friends," she said, in a low voice.

"We can walk away," replied the officer, and turned his face in the opposite direction. "It is too late; and, besides, why should we?" And Mae looked full in his face, then turned to the carriage, which was close upon them.

"How do you all do?" she cried, gleefully and bravely. "Isn't there room for me in there? Mrs. Jerrold, I would like to introduce Signor—your name?"—she said, quite clearly, in Italian, turning to the officer.

"Bero," he replied.

"Signor Bero. He was very kind, and saved me from—from a little beggar boy."

"You must have been in peril, indeed," remarked Mrs. Jerrold, bowing distantly to Bero, and beckoning the coachman, as Mae sprang into the carriage, to drive on. "I am sorry to put you on the box, Norman," Mrs. Jerrold added, as Mae took the seat, in silence, that Mr. Mann had vacated for her, "and I hope Miss

Mae is also." But Mae didn't hear this. She was plucking up courage in her heart, and assuming a saucy enough expression, that sat well on her bright face. Indeed, she was a pretty picture, as she sat erect, with lips and nostrils a trifle distended, and her head a little in the air. The Italian thought so, as he walked away, smiling softly, clicking his spurs and stroking his moustache; and Norman Mann thought so too, as he tapped his cane restlessly on the dash-board and scowled at the left ear of the off horse. The party preserved an amazed and stiff silence, as they drove homeward.

"Eric," cried Norman, very late that same night. "Do be sober, I have something to say to you about Miss Mae."

"Norman, old boy, how can a fellow of my make be sober when he has drunk four glasses of wine, waltzed fifteen times, and torn six flounces from a Paris dress? Why, man, I am delirious, I am. Tra, la, la, tra, la, la. Oh, Norman, if you could have heard that waltz," and Eric seized his companion in his big arms and started about the room in a mad dance. "You are Miss Hopkins, Norman, you are Here goes— " but Norman struck out a bold stroke that nearly staggered Eric and broke loose. " For Heaven's sake, Eric, stop this fooling; I want to speak to you earnestly."

"Evidently," replied Eric, with excited face, "forcibly also. Blows belong after words, not before," and the big boy tramped indignantly off to bed.

Norman Mann was in earnest truly, forcible also, for he opened his mouth to let out a very expressive word as Eric left the room. It did him good seemingly, for he strode up and down more quietly. At last he sat down and began to talk with himself. "Norman Mann, you've got to do it all alone," he said. " Albert and Edith and Aunt Martha are too vexed and shocked to do the little rebel any good. Ric, oh, dear, Ric is a silly boy, God bless him, and here I am doomed to make that child hate me, and with no possible authority over her, or power, for that matter, trying to keep her from something terribly wild. If they don't look out, she will break loose. I know her well, and there's strong character under this storm a-top, if only some one could get at it. Damn it." Norman grew forcible again. " Why can't I keep my silly eyes away from her, and go off with the fellows. You see," continued Norman, still addressing his patient double, "she is a rebel, and—pshaw, I dare say it is half my fancy, but I hate that long moustached officer. I wish he would be summoned to the front and be shot. O, I forgot, there's no war. Well, then, I wish he would fall in love with any body but Mae. It must be late. Ric didn't leave that little party very early, I'm sure, but I can't sleep. I'll get down my Sismondi and read awhile. I wonder if that child is feeling badly now. I half believe she is—but here's my book."

Yes, Mae was feeling badly, heart-brokenly, all alone in her room. After a long, harrowing talk with Mrs. Jerrold, at the close of which she had received commands never to go out alone in Rome, because it wasn't proper, she had been allowed to depart for her own room. Here she closed the door leading into Mrs. Jerrold's and Edith's apartment, and opened her window wide, and held her head out in the night air—the poisonous Roman air. The street was very quiet. Now and then some late wayfarer passed under the light at the corner, but Mae had, on the whole, a desolate outlook—high, dark buildings opposite, and black clouds above, with only here and there a star peeping through.

She had taken down her long hair, thrown off her dress, and half wrapped herself in a shawl, out of which her bare arms stretched as she leaned on the deep window seat. She looked like the first woman—of the Darwinian, not the Biblical, Creation. There was a wild, half-hunted expression on her face that was like the set air of an animal brought suddenly to bay. She thought in little jerks, quick sentences that were almost like the barking growls with which a beast lashes itself to greater fury.

"They treated me unfairly. They had no right. I shall choose my own friends. How dare they accuse me of flirting? I flirt, pah! I'd like to run away. This stupid, stupid life!" And so on till the sentences grew more human. "I suppose Mr. Mann thinks I am horrid, but I don't care. I wish I could see Eric, he wouldn't blame me so. What a goose I am to mind anyway. The Carnival is coming! Even these old tombs must give way for ten whole riotous days. I must make them madly merry days. I wonder how I will look in my domino. I suppose the pink one is mine."

So Miss Mae dried her eyes, picked her deshabille self from the window seat, turned up the light, slipped into her pink and white carnival attire, and walked to the window again.

"This is the Corso all full of people, and I'll pelt them merrily, so, and so, and so!" She reached forth her bare, round arm into the darkness, and looked down, where, full under the street light, gazing up at her, stood the Piedmontese officer.

It was at that very moment that Norman Mann put down his Sismondi, and looked from his window also.

CHAPTER IV.

MAE met Mr. Mann at the breakfast table the next morning without the least embarrassment. Indeed, the little flutter in her talk could easily be attributed to unusually high spirits and an excited and pleased fancy. That was how Norman Mann translated it, of course. Really, the flutter was a genuine stirring of her heart with inquietude, timidity and semi-repentance; but Mae couldn't say this, and it's only what one says out that can be reckoned on in this world. So Norman Mann, who saw only the bright cheeks and eyes and restless quickening of an eager girl and did not see the palpitating feminine heart inside, was displeased and half-cold.

Could any one be long cold to Mae Madden? She believed not. She was quite accustomed to lightning-like white heats of anger in those with whom she came in contact, but coldness was out of her line. Still she met the occasion well. "Shall I give you some coffee?" she asked, pleasantly. "We breakfast all alone, until Eric appears. Mrs. Jerrold is not well, and Edith and Albert are off for Frascati."

"Poor child; how much alone she is," he thought to himself.

"I understand we all go to the play to-night?" queried Mae.

"The thought of Shakspeare dressed in Italian is not pleasant to me," said Mr. Mann, after a silence of a few minutes.

"I am quite longing to see him in his new clothes. There is so much softness and beauty in Italian that I expect to gain new ideas from hearing the play robed in more flowing phrases. Shakspeare certainly is for all the world."

"But Shakspeare's words are so strongly chosen that they are a great element in his great plays. And a translation at best is something of a parody, especially a translation from a northern tongue, with its force and backbone, so to speak, into a southern, serpentine, gliding language. You have heard the absurd rendering of that passage from Macbeth where the witches salute him with 'Hail to thee, Macbeth! Hail to thee, Thane of Cawdor!' into such French as '*Comment vous portez vous, Monsieur Macbeth; comment vous portez vous, Monsieur Thane de Cawdor!*' A translation must pass through the medium of another mind, and other minds like Shakspeare's are hard to find."

Norman spoke with so much reverence for Mae's greatest idol that her heart warmed and she smiled approval, though for argument's sake she remained on the other side.

"Isn't a translation more like an engraver's art, and aren't fine engravings to be sought and admired even when we know the great original in its glory of color? Then all writing is only translation, not copying. Shakspeare had to translate the tongues he found in stones, the books he found in brooks, with twenty-six little characters and his great mind, into what we all study, and love, and strive after. But he had to use these twenty-six characters in certain hard, Anglo-Saxon forms and confine himself to them. When he wanted to talk about

"fen-sucked fogs,"

and such damp, shivery places, he is all right, but when he sings of 'love's light wings,' and all that nonsense, he is impeded; now open to him 'Italian, the language of angels'—you know the old rhyme—and see what a chance he has among the "liquid l's and bell-voiced m's and crushed tz's." To-night you will hear

Desdemona call Othello 'Il mio marito,' in a way that will start the tears. What are the stiff English words to that? 'My husband!' Husband is a very uneuphonious name, I think."

Norman Mann smiled. "Another cup of coffee, if you please—not quite as sweet as the last," and he passed his cup. "I believe there is always a charm in a novel word that has not been commonized by the crowd. 'Dear' means very little to us nowadays, because every school girl is every other school girl's 'dear,' and elderly ladies 'my dear' the world at large, in a pretty and benevolent way. So with the words 'husband' and 'wife'; we hear them every day in commonest speech—'the coachman and his wife,' or 'Sally Jones's husband,'—but I take it this is when we stand outside. That wonderful little possessive pronoun *my* has a great, thrilling power. 'My husband' will be as fine to your ears as 'il mio marito,' which has, after all, a slippery, uncertain sound; and as for 'my wife'—"

At that moment the coffee cup, which was on its way back, had reached the middle of the table, where by right it should have been met and guided by the steadier, masculine hand; Norman's hand was there in readiness, but instead of gently removing the cup from Mae's clasp, it folded itself involuntarily about the white, round wrist, as he paused on these last words. Was it the little possessive pronoun that sent the sudden thrill through the unexpecting wrist? At any rate it trembled; the cup, the saucer, the coffee, the spoon, followed a well known precedent, and "went to pieces all at once;" "all at once and nothing first just as bubbles do when they burst." And so alas! did the conversation, and that burst a beautiful bubble Norman had just blown.

Damages were barely repaired when Eric entered the breakfast room with a petulant sort of face and flung himself into a chair. "My! what a head I have on me this morning," he groaned. "Soda water would be worth all the coffee in the world, Mae; I'll take it black, if you please. How cosy you two look. I always take too much of every thing at a party, from flirtation to— O, Mae, you needn't look so sad. I'm not the one in disgrace now. Mrs. Jerrold, Edith and Albert are just piping mad at you, and as for Mann, here,—by the way," and Eric rubbed his forehead, as if trying to sharpen up a still sleepy memory, "I suppose you two have had it out by this time. Norman sat up till ever so late to talk you over with me, Mae. Do thank him for me ; I am under the impression that I didn't do so last night."

Mae tapped her fourth finger, on which a small ring glistened, sharply against the cream jug. "If I were every body's pet lamb or black sheep, I couldn't have more shepherd's crooks about me. Have you joined the laudable band, Mr. Mann, and am I requested to thank you for that? "

"Not at all. Perhaps your brother's remembrances of last night are not very distinct. I certainly sat up for Sismondi's sake, not for yours." And he really thought, for the moment, that he told the truth.

"I warn you," continued Mae, rising as she spoke, "that I have a tremendous retinue of mentors; and nurses, and governesses already. You had better content yourself with the fact that you have four proper traveling companions, and bear the disgrace of being shocked as best you may by one wild scrap of femininity who will have her own way in spite of you all." Mae half laughed, but she was serious, and the boys both knew it.

"You flatter me," replied Norman. "I had

aspired to no such position, but for your brother's sake, if not for your own, I wished to tell Eric that the Roman air at midnight was dangerous to your health. I saw you had your window open."

"Did you look through the ceiling, pray?" Mae retorted from the door-way. "Eric, ring if you want anything. Rosetta is close at hand."

"I have put my foot in it this time," said Eric, clumsily. "I am real sorry, Norman, old boy."

Norman did not feel like being pitied, and this remark of Eric's roused him. He fairly ground his teeth and clenched his hands, but his big brown moustache and the tablecloth hid these outer manifestations of anger. "Don't be a goose, Ric," he said. "What possible difference can all this make to me? Your sister is young and quick."

Now, it was Eric's turn to wince. Was he giving this fellow the impression that he thought his sister's opinions would affect him? Horrible suspicion! Boys always fancy everybody in love with their sister. He must cure that at once. "Of course," he replied quickly, "I know you and Mae never agree, that you barely stand each other. But

I didn't know but you would prefer to be on good terms with her, for all that."

"Miss Mae can choose the terms on which we meet. I shall be content whatever her decision. What are your plans for the day?"

Lounging Eric straightened himself at once. "I was a perfect fool last night," he confessed, "and I must rely on you, old fellow, to help me out. I made engagements for two weeks ahead with Miss Hopkins and Miss Rae. At any rate, I'm booked for the play to-night. Now, I can't take two girls very well. That is, I can, but I thought you might like a show. You may have your choice of the two. Miss Rae, by the way, says she's wild to know you; thought you were the most provoking man she ever saw; and that you were—nonsensical idea—engaged to Mae. All because you wouldn't look at her the other day when she passed you two. But you can go with Miss Hopkins, if you prefer."

"Are they pretty?" asked Norman, apparently warming to the task, "and bright?"

"I should say they were. Miss Hopkins has gorgeous great eyes,—but Miss Rae is more your style. Still, you may have your choice."

"Silly boy; you're afraid to death that I

shall choose Miss Hopkins. Well, if they are not over stupid and flirtatious—"

"Stupid! Oh, no,"—Eric scouted that idea—"and flirtatious, perhaps. Miss Hopkins rolls her eyes a good deal, but then she has a frankness, a winning way."

"Well," laughed Norman, "you're such a transparent, susceptible infant-in-arms that I'll go with you."

"As shepherd," suggested Eric, "as long as Mae won't have you. But come, we must go down and call on these people. It won't do at all for you to appear suddenly this evening, and say, 'I'll relieve my friend here of one of you.'"

"Oh, what a bore. Is that necessary? Won't a card or a box of Stillman's bon-bons do them? Well, if it must be, come along, then."

CHAPTER V.

IT was evening, and the brilliantly lighted theatre was crowded to overflowing. Of course there were English who scowled at the Americans, and Americans who smiled on every one and ate candy while Othello writhed in jealous rage, and a scattering of Germans with spectacles and a row of double-barrelled field glasses glued over them, and Frenchmen with impudent eyes and elegant gloves, and a general filling in of Italians, with the glitter here and there of nobility, and still oftener of bright uniforms. Finally there was a modicum of true gentry, and these not of any particular nation or class. It is pleasant to name our party immediately after referring to these goodly folks. They had a fine box, and although their ranks were thinned by the loss of two cavaliers, nobody seemed to care. Albert and Edith were perfectly happy side by side, and Mrs. Jerrold was well contented to observe her daughter's smile as Albert spoke to her, and the look of manly protection in his eyes, as his gaze met Edith's.

As for Mae, she had that delicious feminine pride which is as good a stimulant as success to women—in emergencies. And to-night was an emergency to this small, excitable, young thing. Her eyes were very dark from the expansion of the pupil. They possessed a rare charm, caught from a trick the eyelids had of drooping slowly and then suddenly and unexpectedly lifting to reveal the wide, bright depths, that half-concealed, half-revealed power, which is so tantalizing. Mae was dressed in this same spirit to-night, and she was dimly conscious of it. The masses of tulle that floated from her opera hat to her chin and down on her shoulders, revealed only here and there a glimpse of rich brown hair, or of white throat. Her cheeks were scarlet, her lips a-quiver with excitement and pleasure. She formed a pretty contrast to Edith, who sat by her side. Miss Jerrold leaned back in her chair quietly, composedly. She fanned herself in long sweeps, looked pleased, contented, but in no wise displaced or surprised—thoroughly well-bred and at home. She might have had a private rehearsal of Othello in her own dramatic hall the evening before, from her air and mien. Mae, on the contrary, was alert, on the *qui vive*, as interested as a child in each newcomer, and, after the curtain rose, in every tableau.

Such a woman can not fail to attract attention, as long as she is herself unconscious. The world grows *blasé* so speedily that it enjoys all the more thoroughly the sight of freshness, verve, life,—that is, the male portion of the world. Women's great desire, as a rule, is to appear entirely at ease, city-bred, highbred, used to all things, surprised by none.

So there were a great many glasses turned toward Mae that evening. Very probably the young women in the next box accepted a share of these glances as their own, and, in a crowd where the French and Italian elements predominate, or largely enter, they could not have been far wrong. Every girl or woman who pretends to any possible charm is quite sure of her share of admiration from these susceptible beings. The young ladies of the next box had that indescribable New York air, which extends from the carefully brushed eyebrows quite to the curves of the wrist and hand. Praise Parisian modes all you will, but for genuine style, a New York girl, softened a trifle by commonsense or good taste, leads the world—certainly if she is abroad. For there she soon finds it impossible to go to the extremes that American air seems to rush her into. Three months, or perhaps, if she is observant, three days in Paris, teach her that the very biggest buttons, or the very largest paniers, or the very flaringest hats are not for her, or any lady, and by stepping back to size number two, she does not detract from her style, while she does add to her lady-likeness.

These two girls, it may be surmised, were no other than Miss Hopkins and Miss Rae, whom chance or fate or bungling Eric Madden, who bought the tickets, had seated side by side with the Maddens and Jerrolds. It was bothersome, when Norman and Eric had played truant at any rate, but there was no help for it; so after a little Eric introduced them all round, and the two parties apparently merged into one, or broke up into four, for *tête-à-têtes* soon began. It was a little hard that three girls should have each a devoted servant, and that only one, and that one, Mae, should be obliged to receive her care from the chaperon; but so it was.

Nevertheless, Mae bore herself proudly. She was seated next Miss Rae, separated only by the nominal barrier of a little railing, while just beyond sat Norman, his chair turned toward the two girls. The stranger insisted on drawing Mae into the conversation, partly for curiosity's sake, to watch her odd face and manners, partly from that genuine generosity that comes to the most selfish of women, when she is satisfied with her position. It is pleasant to pity, to be generous; and Miss Rae, having the man, could afford to share him now and then, when it pleased her, with the lonely girl by her side. But Miss Rae's tactics did not work. Mae replied pleasantly when addressed, but returned speedily and eagerly to Mrs. Jerrold or a survey of the house, with the frank happiness of a child. She was all the more fascinating to the admiring eyes that watched her, because she sat alone, electrified by the inspiration and magnetism from within, and did not need the stimulus of another voice close by her side, breathing compliments and flattery, to brighten her eyes and call the blushes to her cheeks. Norman Mann saw the eyes fixed on her, and they vexed him. At the same time, he liked her the better on that very account.

And at last the curtain rose.

It was just as Desdemona assures her father of her love for Othello, that Mae became conscious of a riveted gaze—of a presence. Lifting her eyes, and widening them, she looked over to the opposite side of the house, and there, of course, was the Piedmontese officer again, handsomer, more brilliant than ever, with a grateful, soft look of recognition in his eyes.

Mae was out of harmony with all her friends. She was proud and lonely. The man's pleased, softened look touched her heart strangely. There was almost a choke in her throat, there were almost tears in her eyes, and there was a free, glad, welcoming smile on her lips.

Norman Mann saw it and followed it, and caught the officer receiving it, and thought "She's a wild coquette."

And Mae knew what he saw and what he thought.

Then a strange spirit entered the girl. Here was a man who vexed her, who piqued her, and who was rude, for Mae secretly thought it was rude to neglect Mrs. Jerrold, as the boys did that evening, and yet who was vexed and piqued in his turn, if she did what he didn't like and looked at another man.

And then here was the other man. Mae looked down at him.

Bless us! who is to blame a young woman

for forgetting everything but the "other man" when he is a godlike Piedmontese officer, with strong soft cheek and throat, and Italian eyes, and yellow moustaches, and spurs and buttons that click and shine in a maddening sort of way?

Of course, in reality, everybody is to blame her, we among the very virtuous first. In this particular case, however, we have facts, not morals, to deal with. Mae did see Norman Mann talking delightedly to a pretty girl, and she did see the officer gazing at her rapturously, and she quite forgot Othello, and gave back look for look, only more shy and less intense perhaps, and knew that Norman Mann was very angry and she and the officer very happy. What matter though the one should hate her, and the other love her, and she—

But, bother all things but the delirious present moment. Never fear consequences. There were bright lights, and brilliant people, the hum of many voices, the flash of many eyes, and a half secret between her, this little creature up in the box, and the very handsomest man of them all.

So while Othello fell about the stage, and ground out tremendous curses, Mae half shivered and glanced tremblingly toward Bero, and Bero gazed back protectingly and grandly. Once, when Desdemona cried out thrillingly, "Othello, il mio marito," Mae looked at Norman involuntarily and caught a half flash of his eye, but he turned back quickly to his companion and Mae's glance wandered on to Bero and rested there as the wild voice cried out again, "il mio marito, il mio marito."

So the evening slid on. Mae smiled and smiled and opened and half closed her eyes, and Norman invited Miss Rae to go to church with him, and to drive with him, and to walk with him, and to go to the galleries with him, "until, Susie Hopkins, if you will believe it, I fairly thought he would drop on his knees and ask me to go through life with him, right then and there." So Miss Rae confided to Susie Hopkins after the victorious night, in the silence of a fourth-story Costanzi bedroom.

Susie Hopkins was putting her hair up on crimping-pins, but she paused long enough to say: "Well, Jack Durkee had better hurry himself and his ring along, then."

"O, he's coming as quickly as ever he can," laughed Miss Rae, whereat she proceeded to place a large letter and a picture under the left-hand pillow, crimped her hair, cold-creamed her lips, and laid her down to pleasant dreams of—Jack.

CHAPTER VI.

AE was very much ashamed of herself the next morning. She had been restored in a measure to popular favor, through Eric, the day before. Edith and Albert were home from Frascati, when Eric made his raid bravely on their forces combined with those of Mrs. Jerrold. He advanced boldly. "It's all nonsense, child, as she is," he said. "It was natural enough, to talk with the man," for Mae had made a clean breast of her misdoings to him, to the extent of saying that they had chatted after the beggar left. "Do forgive her, poor little proud tot, away across the sea from her mother. Albert, you're as hard as a rock, and that Edith has no spirit in her," he added, under his breath. This remark made Albert white with rage. Nevertheless, he put in a plea for his wayward, reckless little sister, with effect. After a few more remarks from Mrs. Jerrold, Mae came out of the ordeal; was treated naturally, and, as we have seen, accompanied Mrs. Jerrold to the play the night before.

Now, it was the next day. Mrs. Jerrold

breakfasted in her own room again, and spent the hours in writing home letters full of the Peter and Paul reminiscences and quotations. Norman and Eric left for the Costanzi, and Albert and Edith, armed with books, and note-books, and the small camp-stools, again started away together. This last 'again' was getting to be accepted quite as a matter of course. Everybody knew what it meant. They always invited the rest of the company to go with them, and were especially urgent, this morning, that Mae should accompany them.

"Why, with mamma in her room you will be lonely," suggested Edith, "and you can't go out by yourself."

Mae winced inwardly at this, but replied pleasantly: "I have letters to write also, and I'm not in the mood to-day for pictures, and the cold, chilling galleries filled with the damp breath of the ages."

So Edith and Albert, nothing loth, having discharged their duty, started off. These two have as yet appeared only in the background, and may have assumed a half-priggish air in opposition and contrast to Mae. They really, however, were very interesting young people. Albert with a strong desire in his heart—or was it in his head?—to aid the world, and Edith with a clear self-possession and New England shrewdness that helped and pleased him. Their travels were enriching them both. Edith was trying to draw the soul from all the great pictures and some of the lesser ones, and Albert was waking, through her influence, to the world of art. This morning they were on their way to the Transfiguration to study the scornful sister. They were taking the picture bit by bit, color by color, face by face. There are advantages in this analytical study, yet there is a chance of losing the spirit of the whole. So Mae thought and said: "I know that sister now, Edith, better than you ever will." This was while she was looping up her friend's dress here, and pulling out a fold there, in that destructive way girls have of beautifying each other. "See here!"

And down sank Miss Mae on her knees, with her lips curved, and her hands stretched out imploringly, half-mockingly. No need of words to say: "Save my brother, behold him. Ah, you cannot do it, your power is boast. Yet, save him, pray."

"A little more yellow in my hair, some pearls and a pink gown, and you might have the sister to study in a living model, Edith," laughed Mae, arising.

Edith and Albert were both struck by Mae's dramatic force, and they talked of her as they drove to the Vatican. "I wish I understood her better," said Edith. "I cannot feel as if travel were doing her good. She is changing so; she was always odd, but then she was always happy. Now she has her moods, and there is a look in her eye I am afraid of. It is almost savage. You would think the beauty in Rome would delight her nature, for she craves beauty and poetry in everything. I don't believe the theatre is good for her. Albert, suppose we give up our tickets for Thursday night."

"But you want particularly to see that play, Edith."

"I can easily give it up for Mae's sake. It would be cruel to go without her, and I think excitement is bad for her."

"You are very generous, Edith, and right, too, I dare say. I wish my little sister could see pleasure and duty through your steadier, clearer eyes."

Then the steady, clear eyes dropped suddenly, and the two forgot all about Mae, and rolled contentedly off, behind the limping Italian horse. And the red-cheeked *vetturino* with the flower in his button-hole, whistled a love-song, and thought of his Piametta, I suppose.

Meantime, Mae, left to herself, grew penitent and reckless by turns, blushed alternately with shame and with quick pulse-beats, as she remembered Norman Mann's face, or the officer's smile. She wondered where he lived, and whether she would see him soon again. Poor child! She was really innocent, and only dimly surmised how he would haunt her hereafter. Would he look well in citizen's clothes? How would Norman Mann seem in his uniform? She wished she had a jacket cut like his. And so on in an indolent way. But penitence was getting the better of her, and after vainly trying to read or write, she settled herself down for a cry. To think that she, Mae Madden, could have acted so absurdly. She never would forgive herself, never. Then she cried some more, a good deal more.

About four in the afternoon a very bright sunbeam peeped through her closed blinds, and she brushed away her tears, and peace came back to her small heart, and she felt like a New England valley after a shower, very fresh and clean, and goodly,—just] a trifle subdued, however.

She would go to church. She had heard that there was lovely music at vespers, in the little church at the foot of Capo le Case. St. Andrea delle Frate, was it? It wasn't very far away. She could say her prayers and repent entirely and wholly. So she dressed rapidly, singing the familiar old Te Deum joyously all the while, and off she started.

The air was cool and clear and delicious and the street-scenes were pretty. Mae took in everything before her as she left the house, from the Barberini fountain to the groups of models at the corner of the Square and the Via Felice; but she did not see, at some distance behind her, on the opposite side of the street, the sudden start of a motionless figure as she left the house, or know that it straightened itself and moved along as she did, turning on to the pretty Via Sistina, so down the hill at Capo le Case, to the church below.

She was early for vespers, and there was only the music singing in her own happy little heart as she entered the quiet place. The contrast between the spot, with its shrines and symbols and aids to faith, and all that she had associated with religion, conspired to separate her from herself and her past, and left her a bit of breathing, worshiping life, praising the great Giver of Life. She fell on her knees in an exalted, jubilate spirit. She was more like a Praise-the-Lord psalm of David than like a young girl of the nineteenth century.

And yet close behind her, a little to the left, was Bero on his knees too, at his pater nosters.

By and by the music began. It was music beyond description; those wonderful male voices, the chorus of young boys, and then suddenly, the organ and some one wild falsetto carrying the great Latin soul-laden words up higher.

All this while Mae's head was bent low and her heart was a-praying.

All this while Bero was on his knees also, but his eyes were on Mae.

The music ceased; the prayers were ended. Mae heard indistinctly the sweep of trailing skirts, the sound of footsteps on the marble floor, the noise of voices as the people went away, but still she did not move. The selah pause had come after the psalm.

When she did rise, and turn, and start to go, her eyes fell on the kneeling form. She tried to pass quickly without recognition, but he reached out his hand.

"This is a church," said Mae; "my prayers are sacred; do not disturb me."

He held his rosary toward her, with the cross at the end tightly clasped in his hand. "My prayers are here, too," he said. "Oh, Signorina, give me one little prayer, one of your little prayers."

He knelt before her in the quiet, dim, half light, his hands clasped, and an intense earnestness in his easily moved Italian soul, that floated up to his face. It looked like beautiful penitence and faith to Mae. Here was a soul in sympathy with hers, one which met her harmoniously in every mood, slid into her dreams and wild wishes, sparkled with her enjoyment, and now knelt as she knelt, and asked for one of her prayers.

She stood a minute irresolute. Then she smiled down on him a full, rich smile, and said in English: "God bless you." The next moment she was gone.

Bero made no movement to follow her, but remained quietly on his knees, his head bowed low.

* * * * * * *

"I looked in at St. Andrea's, at vespers," said that dear, bungling fellow, Eric, at dinner that night, "and saw you Mae, but you were so busy with your prayers I came away." There was a pause, and Mae knew that people looked at her.

"Yes, I was there; the music was wonderful."

"Mae," asked Mrs. Jerrold, "Do you have to go to a Roman Catholic Church to say your prayers?" For Mrs. Jerrold was a Puritan of the Puritans, and had breathed in the shorter catechism and the doctrine of election with the mountain air and sea-salt of her childhood. Possibly the two former had had as much to do as the latter with her angularity and severe strength.

"Indeed," cried Mae, impulsively, "I wish I could always enter a church to say my prayers. There is so much to help one there."

"Is there any danger of your becoming a Romanist?" enquired Mrs. Jerrold, pushing the matter further.

"I wish there were a chance of my becoming anything half as good, but I am afraid there isn't. Still, I turn with an occasional loyal heart-beat to the great Mother Church, that the rest of you have all run away from." "Yes, you have," Mae shook her head decidedly at Edith. "She may be a cruel mother. I know you all think she's like the old woman who lived in a shoe, and that she whips her children and sends them supperless to bed, and gives them a stone for bread, but she's the mother of all of us, notwithstanding."

"What a dreadful mixture of Mother Goose and Holy Bible," exclaimed Eric, laughingly, while Mae cooled off, and Mrs. Jerrold stared amazedly, wondering how to take this tirade. She concluded at last that it would be better to let it pass as one of Mae's extravagances, so she ended the conversation by saying: "I hope, Eric, you will wait for your sister, if you see her alone, at church. It is not the thing for her to go by herself."

"No," added Albert, "we shall have to buy a chain for you soon."

"If you do," said Mae quietly, "I'll slip it." And not another prayer did she say that night.

CHAPTER VII.

T was the first day of Carnival. The determination to enjoy herself was so strong in Mae, that her face fairly shone with her "good time coming." She popped her head out of the doorway, and flung a big handful of confetti right at Eric, but he dodged, and Norman Mann caught it in his face. Then, seeing a try-to-be-dignified look creeping upon Mae, he seized the golden moment, gathered up such remnants of confetti as were tangled in his hair and whiskers, and flung them back again, shouting: "Long live King Pasquino! So his reign has begun, has it?"

"Yes; King Pasquino is lord, now, for ten whole days," and she slowly edged her right hand about, to take aim again at Norman. He saw her, and frustrated the attempt by catching it and emptying the contents out upon the floor. The little white balls rolled off to the corners and the little hand fell slowly by Mae's side. "Why not go down to the Corso, you and I, and see the beginning of the fun?" suggested Norman.

"Come along," cried Mae, "you, too, Eric," and the three started off like veritable children, in a delightful, familiar, old-time way. Arrived at their loggia, they found an old woman employed in filling, with confetti, a long line of boxes, fastened to the balustrade of the balcony. Little shovels, also, were provided, for dealing out the tiny missals of war upon the heads below. There were masks in waiting, some to be tied on, while others terminated in a handle, by a skilful use of which they could be made as effective as a Spanish lady's fan. Mae chose one of these latter.

The Corso was alive with vendors of small bouquets and bon-bons and little flying birds tied in live agony to round yellow oranges. The fruit in turn was fastened to a long pole and so thrust up to the balconies as a tempting bait. If bought, the birds and flowers were tossed together into the streets to a passing friend. As Mae was gazing rapturously over the balcony, laughing at the few stragglers hurrying to the Piazza del Popolo, admiring the bannered balconics and gay streamers, several of these little birds were thrust up to her face, some of them peeping piteously and flapping their poor wings. She put up her hands and caught the oranges, one—two—three—four. In a moment she had freed the fluttering birds and tossed the fruit back into the street. "Pay them, Eric," she cried indignantly; "Why, what is this?" for one of the little creatures, after vainly flapping its wings, had fallen on the balcony. Mae picked it up. It half opened its eyes at her and then lay still in her hands.

"It is dead," said Mae, quietly, going up to Norman. "Oh! Mr. Mann, I thought Carnival meant real fun, not cruelty. Isn't there anywhere in this big world where we can get free from such dreadful things? Well!" she added, impatiently, as Norman paused.

"Give a slow fellow who likes the world better than you do, time to apologize for it," replied Norman, as familiarly as Eric would have done. The tone pleased Mae. She looked up and laughed lightly. "At any rate," suggested he, "let's forget the cruelty now and take the fun. Three of them are safe and very likely this scrap," and he touched the dead bird in her hand, "is flying to rejoin his brothers in hunting-grounds that are stocked with angle-worms, and such game. We are to have a good time to-day, you and I."

At this moment Eric rushed up. "Say, Mann," he cried, "here they come. They have taken the balcony just opposite, after all. And Miss Hopkins looks perfectly in a white veil. And oh! here are the rest of our own party."

Mae lifted her eyes to the opposite side of the street, but they did not fall to the level of the Hopkins-Rae party, being stopped by something above. At a high, fourth-story window, beyond the circle of flying fun and frolic, confetti and flowers, Mae saw a wonderful woman's face, a face with great dark eyes and raven hair. A heavily-figured white lace veil was pulled low over her brow, and fell in folds against her cheeks. Her skin was white, the scarlet of her face concentrating in her lips.

There was a strange consonance between the creamy heavy lace and its flowing intertwined figures, and the face it encircled. A mystery, a grace, a subtle charm, that had the effect of a vivid dream, in its combination of clearness and unreality. There was life, with smothered passion and pride and pain in it, Mae was sure. So near to her that her voice could have arched the little distance easily, and yet so far away from her life and all that touched it.

A gentleman attending the ady whispered

to her. She bent her eyes on Mae, and met her glance with a smile, and Mae smiled rapturously back.

Mae had been looking for Bero all that afternoon. She felt sure he would be there, and very soon she saw him among a crowd of officers sauntering slowly down the Corso. He looked up at the window opposite. The veiled lady leaned slightly forward and bowed and waved her white hand. Bero bowed. So did the other officers.

Norman Mann and Eric excused themselves long enough to dash over to welcome their friends and then stayed on for a little chat. These young women were quite gorgeous in opera cloaks and tiny, nearly invisible, American flags tucked through their belts. They tossed confetti down on every one's heads, and shouted—a little over-enthusiastically, but one can pardon even gush if it is only genuine. That was the question in this case.

The horse race came; and Mae went fairly wild. When it was over, every body prepared to go home. King Pasquino had virtually abdicated in favor of the Dinner Kings. Mae unclasped her tightly strained hands, clambered down from a chair she had perched herself on, smiled a good-bye at the veiled lady, and came away. She rode home quietly with a big bouquet of exquisite blue violets in her hand. There was a rose on top and a fringe of maiden's hair at the edge, and the bouquet was flung from Bero's own hand up at the side window on the quiet Jesu e Maria, when everyone else but Mae was out on the Corso balcony.

"It is dreadful to grow old," said Mae, breaking silence, as the carriage clattered over the stony streets.

"My dear," expostulated Edith, "you surely don't call yourself old. What do you mean?"

"I fancied I could take the Carnival as a child takes a big bonbon and just think with a smack of the lips, 'My! how good this is.' But here I am, wondering what my candy is made of all the time, and forgetting, except at odd moments, to enjoy myself for trying to separate false from true, and gold from gilt. Still, what is the use of this stuff now! I'll remember that horse race, for there I did forget myself and everything but motion. How I would like to be a horse!" And the volatile Mae seized the stems of her bouquet for whip and bridle and gave a little inelegant expressive click-click to her lips as if she were spurring that imaginary steed herself.

Norman smiled. "We can't keep children for ever, even—"

"The silliest of us?"

"Even the freshest and blithest."

"O, dear, that is like a moral to a Sunday-school book," said Mae; "don't be goody-goody to-night."

"What bad thing shall I do to please your majesty, my lady Pasquino?"

"Waltz," said Mae. So, after dinner, Edith and Eric sang, and Norman and Mae took to the poetry of motion as ducks take to water, and outdanced the singers.

"Thank you," said Mae, smiling up at him. "This has done me good." She pushed the brown hair back from her forehead and drew some deep breaths and leaned back in her chair, still tapping her eager, half-tired foot against the floor, while Norman fanned her with his handkerchief.

This time Bero and the strange, veiled lady and Miss Hopkins and every other confusing thought floated off, and left them quite happy for — well — say for ten minutes.

And ten minutes consecutive enjoyment is worth waiting for, old and cynical people say.

* * * * * * * *

The next morning brought back all her troubles, with variations and complications, on account of some more misunderstood words.

"I think," said Mae, as she paused to blot the tenth page of a home letter. "that likes and dislikes are very similar, don't you, Edith?" Then, as Edith did not reply, she glanced up, and saw that her friend's chair was occupied by Norman Mann. He looked up also and smiled.

"I am not Edith, you see, but I am interested in your theory all the same. Only, as I am a man, I shall require you to show up your reasons."

"Well, I find that people who affect me very intensely either way, I always feel intuitively acquainted with. I know what they will think and how they will act under given conditions, and I believe we are driven into friendship or strong dislikes more by the force of circumstances than by—"

"Elective affinities or any of that nonsense," suggested Norman Mann.

"Yes," said Mae, nodding her head, and repeating her original statement under another form, as a sort of conclusion and proof to the conversation. "Yes, a natural acquaintance may develope into your best friend or your worst foe." She started on page number eleven of her letter, dipping her pen deep into the ink-stand and giving such a particular flourish to her right arm, as to nearly upset the bouquet of flowers at her side. It was Bero's gift. Norman Mann put out his hand to save it. His fingers fell in among the soft flowers and touched something stiff. It felt like a little roll of paper. Indignantly and surprisedly he pulled it out. "What is this?" he cried.

Mae sprang forward, her cheeks aflame. "It is mine," she said.

"Did you put it here?" asked Norman.

"No."

"Then how do you know it is yours? Is not this a carnival bouquet, idly tossed from the street to the balcony?"

Mae straightened to her utmost height which wasn't lofty then and said hastily: "Mr. Mann, this is utterly absurd, and more. I am not a child, and if I catch an idly flung bouquet that holds idle secrets, I surely have a right to them." She laughed hurriedly. "Come, give me my note,—some Italian babble, I dare say."

Norman looked at her for a minute with a struggle in his heart and a flash of half scorn, Mae thought, on his face. What was he thinking?

That the child was in danger. He had no doubt in his own mind now that the flowers and the note came from Bero and that Mae knew it. He held the paper crushed in his hand, while he looked at her.

"I presume you will never forgive me," he said, "but I must warn you, not as a mentor or even as a friend," noticing her annoyed air, "but as one soul is bound to warn another soul, seeing it in danger. Take care of yourself, and there!" And taking the crushed note between his two hands, he deliberately tore it asunder and threw the halves on the table before her.

"And there, and there, and there!" cried Mae, tearing the fragments impetuously, and scattering the sudden little snow flakes before him. Then, with a look of supreme contempt, she left the room.

Norman looked down on the white heap that lay peacefully at his feet. "I am a fool," he thought.

"Little Mae Madden, little Mae Madden, I am so sorry for you," repeated that excited bit of womankind to herself in the silence of her own room. "What won't they drive you to yet? How dreadful they think you are? And only last night we thought things were all coming around beautifully!"

And she looked at herself pityingly in the glass. A mirror is a dangerous thing for a woman who has come to pity herself. She sees the possibilities of her face too clearly. And Mae, looking into the mirror then, realized to an extent she never had before, that her eyes and mouth might be powerful friends to herself and foes to Norman Mann, if she so desired. And to-day she did so desire, and went down to the Carnival with as reckless and dangerous a spirit as good King Pasquino could have asked.

The details of this day were very like those of the last. Norman and Eric vibrated between the Madden and Hopkins balconies; the crowd was great; confetti and flowers filled the air; and up above it all, circled by her crown of misty, heavy lace-work, shone out the beautiful, wonderful face of the strange lady. She dropped smiles from under her long black lashes and from the corners of the rare, sweet mouth over the heads of the idlers to Mae, who looked up to catch them. There was a resting, almost saving influence, Mae's excited soul believed, in the strange face; and her eyes sought it constantly. She had been quite oblivious to the friends about this beautiful stranger, but once, as her eyes sought the Italian's, she saw her arise with a sudden flash of light on her face, and hold out a white hand. A head bent over it, and as it lifted itself slowly, Mae saw once more the well-known features of the Signor Bero.

She looked down toward the street quickly and a sharp pain filled her heart.

She had lost her only friend in Rome, so the silly girl said to herself. If he knew that wonderful woman, and if she flashed those weary, great eyes for him, how could he see or think of any other? Moreover, it was very vexatious to have him there. If she smiled up at the girl, Bero might think she was watching him, trying to attract his notice. So Mae appeared very careless and played she did not see him at all, at all. Yet she could not resist looking up now and then for one of the rare smiles. They seemed like very far between "nows and thens" to Mae, averaging possibly a distance of four minutes apart. But that is as one counts time by steady clock-ticks, and not by heart-beats.

Meanwhile, what could she do with her eyes? They would wander once in a while over to the opposite balcony, at just such moments as when Norman Mann was picking up Miss Rae's fan and receiving her thanks for it from under her drooped eyelids, or choosing a flower for himself, "the very, very prettiest, Mr. Mann," before she threw the rest to the winds and the passing gallants.

As Mae grew reckless her eyes grew bright. There were few passers-by who were not attracted by the flash of those eyes. The sailor lads, as they trundled past in their ship on wheels, left the barrels of lime from which they had been pelting the pleasure-seekers to throw whole handfuls of flowers up to the Jesu e Maria balcony; a set of hale young Englishmen picked out their prettiest bonbons for the same purpose; and one elderly, pompous man, who drove unmasked and with staring opera glasses up and down the Corso, quite showered her with bouquets, which he threw so poorly, and with such a shaky old hand, that the street gamins caught them all except such as he craftily flung so that they might assuredly tumble back to the carriage again. And Mae, though she had felt the pleased gaze of a good many eyes before, had never quite put its meaning plainly to herself. She was apt, on such occasions, to feel high-spirited, excited, joyous, but now she realized well that she was being admired, and she led on for victory ardently.

She tossed back little sprays of flowers, or quiet bonbons, or now and then mischievously let drop a sprinkling of confetti balls through her half-closed fingers. To do this she drooped her hand low over among the balcony trimmings, following the soft shower with her eyes, as some straight soldier would wipe the tiny minie balls from his face and glance up to see where they came from. If he looked up once, he never failed to look again, and generally darted around the nearest corner to return with his offering, in the shape of flowers or other pretty carnival nonsense. Mae rather satisfied her conscience, which was tolerably fast asleep for the time being, at any rate, with the fact that she didn't smile at these strangers—she only looked!

Her pleasure wss heightened by the knowledge that she was watched. If she glanced across quickly, Miss Rae's eyes were invariably fixed on her and Norman Mann would be gazing in the opposite direction in the most suspicious manner. From above her strange friend leaned over admiringly and once, as Mae looked joyously upwards, clapped her white hands softly together, while beyond her a tall figure stood motionless. Mae had pretended not to see Bero yet, but as the Italian applauded her in this gentle manner, her eyes sought his involuntarily. He was gazing very fixedly and rapturously down on her, without any apparent thought of the beautiful girl by his side. After that, Mae looked up often, in a glad, childlike way, for spite of this first lesson in wholesale coquetry, and the new conflict of emotions within her mind, she was enjoying herself with the utter abandon of her glad nature.

Toward the close of the afternoon, the Italian was suddenly surrounded by a great mass of flowers, over which she waved her hand caressingly and pointed down at Mae. "For you," the gesture seemed to say. The veiled lady appeared to summon several of her friends, for a number of gentlemen left the other window and its group of girls, and began the difficult task of attempting to toss the bouquets from their height down to Mae. This was rendered the more difficult as the Madden balcony was covered, and the best shots succeeded in landing their trophies on this awning, where they were speedily captured and drawn in by the occupants of the next flat, an ogre of an old woman and her hook-nosed daughter, who wore an ugly green dress and was otherwise unattractive.

The entire Madden party became interested and stood looking on with the most encouraging smiles. The very last bouquet was vainly thrown, however, and gathered in by the ogre, when Bero suddenly appeared, a little behind the party in the window. The flowers in his hand were of the same specimens as those he had given Mae the day before, although different in arrangement. He lifted the bouquet quickly to his lips, so quickly that perhaps only Mae understood the motion, and flung it lightly forward. Mae leaned over the balcony, reaching out her eager hands, and caught it in her very finger tips. The party above bowed and applauded, as she raised the flowers triumphantly to her face.

So the second day of the Carnival was a success, till they turned their backs on the Corso. In the carriage Mrs. Jerrold spoke gently but firmly to Mae. "Be a little more careful, dear; don't let your spirits carry you quite away during these mad days." Mae smiled, but was silent.

"What a strangely beautiful girl that was in the gallery opposite," Edith said, a moment later. "I wonder if she is engaged to that superb man; I fancied I had seen him before. Why, Mae, what in the world are you blushing at?" For Mae's face was scarlet. "Why, nothing," replied Mae, redder yet; "nothing at all. What do you mean?"

The same thought occurred to Edith and Albert. The officer was Mae's chance acquaintance. They both looked grave, and Albert remarked: "It is as well to be careful before getting up too sudden an acquaintance with your Italian girl. Take care of your eyes."

"Has it come to this?" cried Mae, half jestingly, half bitterly. "Are not my very eyes my own? I shall feel, Albert, as if you were trying to bind me in that chain you threatened," and Mae started: her fingers had felt another scrap of paper among the flowers, but she did not drop it from the carriage, as her first impulse was; she held it tight and close in her warm right hand until she was fairly at home and safe in her own room. Then she opened and read in an Italian hand, "To my little Queen of the Carnival."

Could he have written that as he stood by the wonderful veiled lady, with her white mysterious beauty, with the purple shadows about her dark eyes, while she— and Mae looked in her glass again. What did she see? Certainly a different picture, but a picture for all that. Life and color and youth, a-tremble and a-quiver in every quick movement of her face, in the sudden lifting of the eyelids, the swift turn of the lips, the litheness and carelessness of every motion; above and beyond all, the picture possessed that rare quality which some artist has declared to be the highest beauty, that picturesque charm which shines from within, that magnetic flash and quiver which comes and goes "ere one can say it lightens."

The veiled lady's face was stranger, more mysterious, to an artistic or an imaginative mind; but youth, and intense life, and endless variety usually carry the day with a man's captious heart, and so Bero called Mae

"My little Queen of the Carnival."

CHAPTER VIII.

MAE'S good times were greatly dimmed after this by the thought that she was watched. The bouquets which came daily from Bero troubled her also not a little. They were invariably formed of the same flowers, and might easily attract Edith's attention and possible suspicion. So she stayed home from the Corso one day not long after, when she was in a particularly Corso-Carnival mood. She wandered helplessly about, restless and full of desire to be down at the balcony with the rest. And such a strange thing is the human heart, that it was Norman Mann's face she saw before her constantly, and she found Miss Rae's little twinkling sort of eyes far more haunting than those of her veiled friend.

The rich life in Mae's blood was surging in her veins and must be let off in some way. If she had had her music and a piano she might have thrown her soul into some great flood-waves of harmony. The Farnesina frescoes of Cupid and Psyche over across the Tiber would have helped her, but here she was alone, and so she did what so many "fervent souls" do—scribbled her heart out in a colorful, barbarous rhyme. Mae had ordinarily too good sense for this, too deep a reverence for that world of poetry, at the threshold of which one should bow the knee, and loose the shoe from his foot, and tread softly. She didn't care for this to-day. She plunged boldly in, wrote her verse, copied it, sent it to a Roman English paper, and heard from it again two days later, in the following way.

The entire party were breakfasting together, when Albert suddenly looked up from his paper and laughed. "Look here," he cried. "Here is another of those dreadful imitators of the Pre-Raphaelite school. Hear this from a so-called poem in the morning's journal:

'The gorgeous brown reds
Of the full-throated creatures of song.'"

"I don't see anything bad in that," said Eric, helping himself to another muffin. "What is the matter with you?"

"Matter enough," returned Albert. "Because their masters, sometimes, daub on colors with their full palettes and strong brushes, this feeble herd tag after them and flounder around

in color and passion in a way that is sickening."

"Go on," shouted Eric, "he is our own brother, Mae, after all, you see. Fancy my Lord Utilitarian turning to break a lance in defence of beauty. Edith, you and the picture-galleries are to blame for this."

Mae had been paying great attention to her rolls and coffee, and very little apparently to the conversation, but she spoke eagerly now. "Their masters do not daub. They do hold palettes full of the strongest, richest colors, and dare lay them, in vivid flecks, on their canvas. They do not care if they may offend some modern cultivated eyes, used only to the invisible blues and shadowy greens and that host of cold, lifeless, toneless grays, of refined conventional art. They know well enough that their satisfying reds and browns and golds of rich, free nature will go to the beating hearts of some of us."

Mae had a way of dashing into conversation abruptly, and the Madden family had been brought up on argument and table-talk. So the rest of the party ate their breakfast placidly enough. "Mae's right," said Eric, a trifle grandly, "only, to change the figure of speech for one better fitted for the occasion, they may satiate, though they never starve you. But they are wonderfully fine, sometimes. O, bother, I never can quote, but there is something about 'I will go back to the great sweet mother.'"

"Or this," suggested Mae,

"'And to me thou art matchless and fair
As the tawny sweet twilight, with blended
Sunlight and red stars in her hair.'"

"I love my masters," continued this young enthusiast, "because they fling all rules aside, and cry out as they choose. It is their very heart's blood and the lusty wine of life that they give you, not just a scrap of 'rosemary for remembrance,' and a soothing herb-tea made from the flowers of fancy they have culled from those much travestied, abominable fields of thought."

"And this from a lover of Wordsworth, who holds the 'Daffodils' and 'Lucy' as her chief jewels, and quotes the 'Immortality' perpetually!" cried Eric. "If any body ever wandered up and down those same fields of thought, by more intricate, labyrinthine passages and byways, I'd like to know of him. Talk about soothing herbs, bless me, it's hot catnip-tea, good and strong, that he serves up in half of his strings about—"

"O, Eric, hush," cried Mae, "I am afraid for you with such words on your lips. Think of Ananias."

"Before you children go wandering off on one of your poet fights," broke in Albert, "let me take you to task, Mae, for stealing; that lusty wine you talked of just now is in the poem (?) I hold in my hand."

"Do read it to us," said Edith, "and let us judge for ourselves." So Albert began:

ALL ON A SUMMER'S DAY.

"Far away the mountains rise, purpling and joyous,
Through the half mist of the warm pulsing day, while
nigh
At hand gay birds hang swinging and floating
And waving betwixt earth and sky,
Ringing out from ripe throats
A sensuous trickling of notes,
That fall through the trees,
Till caught by the soft-rocking breeze
They are borne to the ears of the maiden.

Her eyes wander after the sound,
And glimpses she catches along
Through green broad-leaved shadows,
Through sunbeams gold-strong,
Of the gorgeous brown reds of the full-throated crea-
tures of song.
One hand on her brown bosom rests,

Rising and falling with every heart-beat
Of the delicate, slow-swelling breasts.

A lily, proud, all color of amber and wine,
Waves peerless there, by right divine
Queen o'er the moment and place.
As the wind bends her coaxingly,
Brushes softly the maiden's white hand—
That falls with an idle grace,
Listlessly closed at her side—
With a rippling touch, such as the tide,
Rising, leaves on a summer day,
On the quiet shore of some peaceful bay.

There she stands in the heavily-bladed grass,
Under the trumpet-vine,
Drinking long, deep, intoxicate draughts
Of Nature's lusty, live wine.
There he sees her as he approaches;
Then pauses, as full on his ear
There swells, on a sudden, loud and clear,
A wonderful burst of song.

A mad delicious glory; a rainbow rhythm of life,
Strong and young and free, a burst of the senses all astrife,
Each one fighting to be first,
While above, beyond them all,
Loud a woman's heart makes call."

"Now, fire ahead," said Eric, "get your stones ready. Mrs. Jerrold, pray begin; let us put down this young parrot with her 'lusty, live wine.'"

"Her?" exclaimed Edith, "Him, you mean."

"Not a bit of it; a woman wrote that, didn't she?"

Eric was very confident. Norman agreed with him, and he glanced at Mae to discover her opinion. There was a look of secret amusement in her face, and a dim suspicion entered his mind, which decided him to watch her closely.

"Well," said Mrs. Jerrold, "I will be lenient. You children may throw all the stones. It is not poetry to my taste. There's no metre to it, and I should certainly be sorry to think a woman wrote it."

"Why?" asked Mae, quickly, almost commandingly. Norman glanced at her. There was a tiny rosebud on each cheek.

"Because," replied Mrs. Jerrold, "it is too—too what, Edith?"

"Physical, perhaps," suggested Edith.

"It is a satyr-like sort of writing," suggested Norman.

"I should advise this person," said Edith—

"To keep still?" interrupted Eric.

"No, to go to work; that is what he or she needs."

"That is odd advice," said Mae; "suppose she—or he—is young, doesn't know what to do, is a traveler, like ourselves, for instance."

"There are plenty of benevolent schemes in Rome, I am sure," said Edith, a trifle sanctimoniously.

"And there's study," said Albert, "art or history. Think what a chance for studying them one has here. Yes, Edith is right—work or study, and a general shutting up of the fancy is what this mind needs."

"I disagree with you entirely," said Norman with energy. "She needs play, relaxation, freedom." Then he was sorry he had said it; Mae's eyes sparkled so.

"She needs," said Eric, pushing back his chair, "to be married. She is in love. That's what's the matter. Read those two last lines, Albert:

> 'While above, beyond them all,
> Loud a woman's heart makes call.'

"Don't you see?"

"O, wise young man," laughed Edith. But Mae arose. The scarlet buds in her cheeks flamed into full-blown roses. "There speaks the man," she cried passionately, "and pray doesn't a woman's heart ever call for anything but love—aren't life and liberty more than all the love in the world? Oh!" and she stopped abruptly.

"Well, we have wasted more time than is worth while over this young, wild gosling," laughed Albert. "Let us hope she will take our advice."

Mae shook her head involuntarily. There was a smile on Norman Mann's lips.

"Here's health and happiness to the poor child at any rate," he said.

"He pities me," thought Mae, "and I hate him." But then she didn't at all.

Mae wandered off to the kitchen, as usual, that day, for another of Lisetta's stories. The Italian, with her glibness of tongue and ready fund of anecdote, was transformed in her imaginative mind into a veritable improvisatore. Talila was not by any means the only heroine of the little tales. Mae had made the acquaintance of many youths and maidens, and to-day Lisetta, after thinking over her list of important personages, chose the Madre Ilkana as the heroine of the occasion. Mae had already heard one or two amusing incidents connected with this old mother. "I am sure she has a cousin in America," she asserted to-day, before Lisetta began, "for I know her well. She knits all the time, and is as bony as a ledge of rocks, and her eyes are as sharp as her knitting-needles, and her words are the sharpest of all. Her name is Miss Mary Ann Rogers. Is she like the Madre Ilkana?"

Lisetta shook her head. "No, no, Signorina, La Madre is as plump and round as a loaf of bread, and as soft as the butter on it. She has five double chins that she shakes all the while, but then she has stiff bristles, like a man's, growing on them, and her knitting-needles and her words are all sharp as la Signora Maria Anne R-o-o-g-eers, I doubt not. But her eyes! Why, Signorina, she has the evil eye!" This Lisetta said in a whisper,. while Giovanni shrugged his shoulders bravely, and little Roberto cuddled closer to Mae.

"Yes," continued Lisetta, "and so no one knows exactly about her eyes, not daring to look directly into them, but as nearly as I can make out they are black, and have a soft veil over them, so that you would think at first they were just about to cry, when suddenly, fires creep up and burn out the drops, and leave her hot and angry and scorching.

"She must be terrible," cried Mae, with a sudden shrinking.

"She *is* terrible," replied Lisetta, "but then she is very clever. You will see if she is not clever when you hear the story I shall now tell you," and Lisetta laughed, and showed her own one double chin, with its two little round dimples. Then she smoothed down her peasant apron, bade Giovanni leave off pinching Roberto, and commenced.

"The government hates the banditti," began Lisetta, wisely, "and indeed it should," and she looked gravely at Giovanni, "for they are very wild men, who live reckless, bad lives, and steal, and are quite dreadful. But we poor, we do not hate them as the government does, because they are good to us, and do not war with us, and sometimes those we love join them—a brother or a cousin, perhaps"—and Lisetta's black eyes filled, and her lip quivered. "As for the Madre, she loved them all, and said they were all relations.

"At this time of which I speak, the soldiers were chasing and hunting the banditti very hard, and they had been compelled to hide for their lives up among the mountains. There they would have died, had it not been for the peasants, who supplied them with food. Small parties of the bandits would come out for it.

There were two very powerful men of the banditti, who were skirmishing about in this way, not far from the Madre Ilkana's, when they saw two soldiers, in advance of their company, approaching them. The banditti were not afraid for themselves, but they wanted to get back to their friends with the bread and meat, so instead of fighting, they fled to the Madre. She took them in, and bade them be sure they were safe with her. But the soldiers had caught sight of them, and they stopped at every house and enquired and searched for them; and so, soon they came to the Madre Ilkana's. They charged her in the name of the government to give up the banditti in her house. The Madre kept on with her knitting, and told them there were only her two sons in the house, and mothers never gave up their sons to any one.

"'Ha!' laughed one of the soldiers, 'mothers must give up their children to King Death, and it is He who wants your bad boys.' Upon which, the Madre arose and cursed them. Curses are common with us, Signorina, but not La Madre's curses. She talked of their mothers to them, and of their sons, and of the Holy Virgin and child, and she cursed them in the name of all these, if they dared steal her children from her. They should take them over her old dead body, she swore, though her knitting-needles and her eyes were her only weapons, and then she turned her eyes full upon them, with the evil spirit leering and laughing out of them, and the soldiers, one of whom was an officer, fell on their knees and shook like leaves, and prayed her to forgive them; saying that they were sure her boys were good sons, and no banditti. And while they knelt crouching there, La Madre knocked on the floor and in rushed the banditti, armed with great knives. They caught and bound the two soldiers, and took away their weapons, and jumped on their horses, and fled.

"La Madre took her knitting again, and sat down quietly by the side of the bound men, until a half hour later some twelve more soldiers cantered up. As they rode by, all the people came to their doorways, and the soldiers stopped and asked if they had seen two horsemen. Then La Madre gathered up her knitting and went quietly out into the crowd. She made a low bow to the man with the biggest feather in his cap, and she told him her story. 'I have two sons,' she said, 'whom I love so well.' Then she told how the soldiers mistook her sons for banditti, and tried to take them from her in her own house. 'Though I am old, I have a good life among my friends and neighbors here, and I fought a while in my own mind before I said to my sons: Go, my boys, your mother will die for you. But I did it. I bade them bind the soldiers and steal away. Then I sat guarding the men till you came. You will find them safe in my little house there. Now, take me to prison—kill me, but look in my eyes first, and then, whoever lays a hand on me, take La Madre Ilkana's curse.'

"And the people all swore that there were two snakes coiled up in La Madre's eyes then, and they hissed, and struck out with their fiery tongues, and the crowd fell on their knees, and the neighbors all set up a great shout of 'La Madre Ilkana,' so that they quite drowned the voice of the man with the big feather."

"Is that all?" asked Mae, as Lisetta paused. "What did the soldiers do?"

"O, they hired a passing carriage to take the men whose horses were stolen back to Castellamare, and they all cantered off, without saying a word to La Madre, and when they had turned a corner of the road, she began to laugh. O, how she laughed! All the people laughed with her, and the children crowed and the dogs barked, for the rest of that whole day.

"And a neighbor who passed La Madre's at midnight, said she was laughing out loud then."

CHAPTER IX.

"SIGNORINA." Mae was passing down the long hall when she heard the whisper. She turned and saw Lisetta, with shining eyes and pink cheeks, standing at her side. Her pretty plump shoulders were only half covered, and the array of colors about her transformed her into a sort of personified rainbow. This was Lisetta's Carnival attire, and very proud she was of it.

"Why, Lisetta, what do you want, and what makes you so happy?" called Mae.

"O, Signorina, the cousins are here,—and others,—all in mask. They fill Maria's rooms quite full. It is very gay out there, and they all want to see you, Signorina. I have told them how well you speak Italian and how you love Italy, and to-night, they say, you shall be one of us. So come." All this while Lisetta had been leading Mae swiftly down the corridor, until as she said these last words, she reached and pushed open the door. A great shout of laughter greeted Mae's ear, and a pretty picture met her eyes—gaily decked youths and maidens clapping their hands and chattering brightly, while the *padrona* was just entering the opposite doorway, bearing two flasks of native wine, and some glasses.

"'Tis genuine Orvieto," she called out, and this raised another shout. Then she caught sight of Mae and bowed low towards her. "Here is the little foreign lady," she cried, and a dozen pairs of big black eyes were turned eagerly and warmly on Mae. She bowed and smiled at them, and said in pleading tones, "O, pray do not call me the 'little foreign lady' now. Play I am as good an Italian as my heart could wish I were."

This speech was received with new applause, and the *padrona* handed around the glasses saying: "We must drink first to the health of our new Italian. May she never leave us."

"Yes, yes," called Lisetta, lifting high her glass. "Yes, yes," cried all, and Mae drank as heartily as any of them. Then she shook her head and gazed very scornfully down on her dark, stylish clothes. "I am not thoroughly Italian yet," she cried. "Here, and here, and here," cried one and another, proffering bits of their own gay costumes, and in a moment Mae had received all sorts of tributes—a string of red beads from one, a long sash from another, a big-balled stiletto from a third, so that she was able from the gleanings to trim herself up into at least a grotesque and un-American Carnival figure. Then the Italians with their soft tongues began to flatter her.

"How lovely the Signorina would look in a contadina costume—the home costume," said Lisetta gravely. "It is so beautiful, is it not?" And then those two or three privileged ones, who had seen Lisetta's home, went into ecstasies over its many charms. Lisetta, next to the Signorina, was the heroine of the occasion. She was from a distance, was handsome and clever, and the *padrona* gave glowing accounts of her full purse, and two pretty donkeys, and house by the sea.

They had a very gay time. Such singing, and then dancing and frolicking, and such a feline softness in all their gaiety. None of the German or Saxon bullying, and barking and showing of teeth; in no wise a game of dogs, which always ends in a fight; but a truly kittenish play, with sharp claws safely tucked out of sight behind the very softest paws, and a rich, gentle curve of motion, inexpressibly witching to our little northern maiden, who was fast losing her head amid it all. Mae did not reflect that felines are treacherous. She only drew a quick, mental picture of the parlor on the other side of the hall, which she compared to this gay scene. Mrs. Jerrold filling in dull row after row of her elaborate sofa cushion, which was bought in all its gorgeousness of floss fawn's head and bead eyes, Edith and Albert hard at work over their note books, or reading up for the sights of to-morrow, Mr. Mann with his open book also, all quiet and studious. Eric, alone, might be softly whistling, or writing an invitation to Miss Hopkins to climb up St. Peter's dome with him, or to visit the tomb of Cecilia Metella, or the Corso, as the case might be, while here—

As Mae reached this point in her musings, the Italians were forming for a dance, so she sprang up to join them. Two or three peasants from the country south had wandered up with the world to Rome, for Carnival time, then for Lent. They had brought with them their pipes and zitterns. In the mornings they made short pilgrimages, playing in front of the shrines about the city, or roaming out on the campagna to some quiet church. In the evening time they wandered up the stone stairways of the great houses, and paused on the landings before the different homes. If all was still they passed on, but if there was noise, laughter, sound of voices, they laid aside their penitential manner, and struck into dance music, flashing their velvety eyes, and striking pretty attitudes, aided greatly by their Alpine hats and sheep-skins and scarlet-banded stockings.

Three of these peasants had appeared at the *padrona's* doorway, by a sort of magic. They bowed and smiled, and commenced to play. Every one sprang up. "Dance," cried they all, and flew for their partners. Mae found herself in the midst of the crowd, and having the most willing and nimble of feet, she soon toned and coaxed the fashionable waltz on which she had started into accord with the more elastic footsteps of her companion. There was something in the serpentine, winding and unwinding motion, the coaxingness of the steps, that was deliciously intoxicating to Mae. The color came to her cheeks, the smile played around her lips, and when she paused to breathe, she found the Italians showing their white teeth, and clapping their brown hands in her honor, while the tallest musician gazed at her from the dark doorway, with the rapt reverence he gave to all things beautiful and thrilling. She was a new song to him.

"The Signorina is the veriest Italian of us all," cried Lisetta.

"She honors our Italy," called Mae's last partner.

"Her feet are those of a chamois," said one from the north.

"Nay, she flies," replied another.

They all spoke in their earnest manner, and the praises, that fall in fulsome flattery in English, were delicate and stimulating as they slid in soft Italian from their full, red lips. Mae tossed her head carelessly, but she sipped the praises and found them sweet.

"Now for the Tarantella," said the *padrona*, so Lisetta shook her tambourine wildly, and the very prettiest girl of them all, and a big, brown boy (happy fellow!) began that coquettish bit of witchery. The pretty girl tripped around and around and wreathed her arms over her head, and the boy knelt appealingly and sprang up passionately again and again, until the clock struck ten, and the party broke up. Mae shook hands with a new friend. He was a stone-cutter, and was soon to be married, and he poured out all his plans and hopes into her sympathetic ears, and told of his pretty bride to be, and of her dowry. Mae, in turn, sent her love to the happy bride, and took a charm from her watch-chain to go with it, a tiny silver boat, and she sent it with a hope that some day they might both sail over to America. At which the bridegroom shook his head very decidedly, and kissed Mae's hand and bowed himself out. Then, after she had disrobed her of her borrowed plumes, all the others kissed her hand and bowed themselves out, and Roberto and Giovanni awaked, and got up from the corner, and stood on their heads and hallooed as loud as ever they pleased, and the evening was over, and Lisetta and the *padrona* and the boys and Mae were alone.

"Oh, oh, oh," cried Mae, "how perfectly perfect. Do you always have such good times as this?"

"At home, yes," replied Lisetta, folding her hands and smiling. "We have many a play-day on the bay of Naples." Then she roused herself: "Good night, Signorina," she said, "keep your ears open."

Mae had barely reached her room when she appreciated Lisetta's last words. She heard music in the street below. She raised her window; Eric and Norman lifted the parlor window at the same moment. "Come in here," they cried. So in she ran, took a place between them, and they silently listened to the maskers' serenade. The musicians sang at first the gayest of tunes, but suddenly, by some subtile impulse, they changed to quieter minor airs, and sang songs full of tears and passion and love and tènderness. Then they silently turned to go. Norman Mann touched Mae on the shoulder. He handed her a bunch of Carnival flowers. They were Bero's, but she flung them unhesitatingly into the street, leaning far out to watch the singers catch them and separate them in the moonlight. They called out loud their thanks—their *"Grazie, grazie,"* as sweet as any lily just broken from its stem—and as they turned to go Mae saw that each one was decked with a sprig from the bouquet, pulled through his button-hole or the riband of his hat.

Only the tallest musician, who walked somewhat apart, carried his flower tightly clasped in his hand, and now and again he raised it to his lips. He probably dreamed over it that night, and played his dream out in a gentle, wistful, minor adoration before the Madonna at the Quattro Fontane the next morning.

O, the dreams and poems and songs without words that drop into our lives from the sudden flash of stranger eyes, or the accidental touch of an unknown hand, or the tender warmth of a swift smile! And if our eyes, our touch, our smiles may only have floated off in like manner—as dreams and poems and melody—to give added rhythm and harmony to other lives.

Mae drew a long sigh, one of those delightful, contented sighs, with a smile wrapped up in it. "I am glad you are so happy," said Norman Mann, smiling down at her. When Norman spoke like that Mae felt only, O, so very content. She quite forgot all grudges against him; she would have liked just at that moment to have the world stand quite still. This was very different from the ordinary Mae. Usually she longed that it might go faster, and would put her pink and white ear quite close to the brown earth to hear if it were turning as swiftly as ever it could. "I like it to hurry, hurry, hurry," said eager, restless Mae. "I love to live quickly and see what's coming next."

But Mae was not in that mood to-night.

She leaned out of the window all untroubled. If the sun could stand still off behind the world —as he is now—and the moon could stand still right before us—as she is now—and we could stay right here, we three. Why, no, Eric has gone in and is walking up and down nervously. Thus Mae thought, and was quiet. "What are you thinking about?" asked Norman. She told him naturally, with her eyes on his until she reached the words "and we." Then her eyes fell, and she paused.

"Yes," replied Norman, "I have the same feeling," and there was a great deal more on the very tippest tip of his tongue. But Mae turned her face from him slightly; the moon stole softly behind the flimsiest little cloud that any one could have seen through, and he paused, silly fellow. These slight withdrawals, that should have urged him on, deceived him. He stopped, and then he remembered Mae's past doings, her recklessness, her waywardness. It was not time yet to speak what he had in his heart to say, and what quivered on his tongue. So he only asked abruptly: "You will go with me to-morrow night for one of your gayest frolics, will you not? We will go down on the Corso for all the Mocoletti fun. I am very anxious to be in another of your good times."

"O, would you like it?" said Mae; "I am so glad. I should delight in it. It will be almost too good." She stopped abruptly again, and gave him a quick, soft glance, just as the moon rode triumphantly out from behind the filmy, flimsy veil, and shone full down on her eyes and hair. It fell on a bright, round, glistening ball, tucked in among some half curls behind her ear. "What is that?" asked Norman.

"That"—Mae put up her hand and drew it out—"that is my stiletto. I forgot to give it back to Lisetta. It is pretty, isn't it?"

Norman took the long needle from her hand and looked at it. "It is not as pretty as the flowered stiletto. Why didn't you get one of those?"

"Why, do you not know that those are not worn by free maidens? They are one of the added glories of a matron. I like my round, smooth ball a great deal better. It means liberty." And she plunged the steel tremulously back into her hair.

"We had better go in now; this night air is bad for you." The moon blazed scornfully down on Norman Mann as he said this. She had had a wide experience, and had rarely seen such a stupid, cowardly fellow, so she thought. Yet, after all, Norman only acted in self-defense. Here was a girl by his side who gloried, as it seemed to him, in her freedom, and that being so, he must get away as soon as possible from that window, that moon, and that little girl.

"Well, Norman," cried Eric, advancing eagerly as they turned from the window, "when do you really suppose it will come off?"

"Suppose what will come off?" inquired Mae.

"O, I forgot you were here. Well, don't tell any one else. Norman is to fight a duel."

"To fight a duel—and be killed?" gasped Mae.

"You have but a poor opinion of my powers," laughed Norman, "although the German looked a veteran duellist from his scars. His face was fairly embroidered or fancy-worked with red lines. A sort of hem in his nose, and tucks and seams all over his cheeks. Notice my knowledge in this line, Miss Mae. You ought to be ashamed, Eric, to have spoken of it."

"Isn't it all a joke?" asked Mae, pushing her head out of the window again, to hide the sudden white terror in her face. "I didn't suppose

Americans fought duels when they were off pleasuring." This sentence Mae meant to pass as a gay, light, easy speech, to prove that Norman Mann and a duel were not such a very dreadful combination to her feminine mind.

"*No*, it is no joke, but dead earnest," replied Eric. "I am to be his second, and you must keep it a great secret, Mae, till it is all over"

"All over!"—a sudden vision of Norman lying white and motionless with a deep wound across his soft, brown temple. Mae closed her eyes. "I suppose I might as well tell you about it," said Norman, "now that this stupid Eric has let out about the affair, although it may never come to anything. I was dining to-night at a little restaurant on the Felice, a quiet, homelike place, which a good many artists, and especially women, frequent. There is a queer, crazy little American, who thinks herself a painter, and is a harmless lunatic, who is a regular guest at this restaurant. Everybody smiles at her absurdities, but is ready enough to be kind to the poor old creature. To-night, however, I was hardly seated when in came a party of Germans, all in mask and Carnival costume. One of them was arrayed in exact imitation of this old lady. He had on a peaked bonnet and long, black gloves, with dangling fingers, such as she invariably wears. These he waved around mockingly and seating himself opposite her, he followed her every motion. The ladies at the same table rose and went away. Then up gets this big ruffian and sits down on the edge of the old lady's chair. I could stand it no longer, but jumping in front of him, showered down all the heavy talk I knew in German, Italian and French, subsiding at last into my mother tongue, with her appropriate epithets. Having sense enough left to know that he could not reap the full benefit of English, I pulled out my card, wrote my address on it, and threw it on the table, and I rather think that was understood. There's no country that I have heard of where, men don't know what 'we'll fight this out, means." Norman was striding up and down the room now almost as restlessly as Eric had done, but he seated himself again as Mae asked for the rest.

"The rest is very simple, Miss Mae—mere business. I turned to go away, and one of his friends approached me to ask for the name of my second. I gave Eric's here. He bowed and said: 'He shall hear from me this evening,' and I came home. The evening has advanced to midnight, but not a word yet. No, it is not quite eleven, I see."

"You'll have the choice of weapons if they challenge you," said Eric; "you'll take pistols, I suppose? Just think of my living to really assist in a 'pistols-and-coffee-for-two' affair!"

"I daresay it will be coffee for two, served separately, and with no thought of pistols. I don't really believe it will come to anything. There are ways of getting out of it," said Norman, lighting a cigarette.

"Will you refuse to fight?" asked Mae, and her heart, which had been white with fear for Norman the second before, flashed now with quick, red scorn. Even the Huguenot maiden would, after all, have despised her lover if he had quietly allowed her to tie the white handkerchief to his arm. Believe it, she loved him far, far better as she clung to him, pressed closely to his warm, living heart, because she realized in an agony that his honor was strong enough to burst even the tender bonds of her dear love, and that he would break from her round arms to rush into that ghostly, ghastly death-embrace on the morrow, at the dreadful knell of St. Bartholomew bells.

Suppose he had yielded. Suppose we saw him in the picture standing quietly, unresistingly, as her soft fingers bound the white badge, that meant protection and life, to his arm. Would not she, as well as he, have known that it was a badge of cowardice, and that he wore a heart as white?

And afterwards, would she have loved the living man, breathing in air heavy with the hearts' life of his brothers and friends, as she worshiped the dead man, whose cold body rested forever down deep in mother earth's brown, soft bosom, but whose very life of life swelled the great throng of heroes and martyrs who have closed their own eyes upon life's pictures, that those pictures might shine clearer and brighter to other eyes?

If the man had yielded, and the picture showed him thus, would we see the Huguenot lovers adorning half the houses of the land? Most often they are found in that particular corner of the home belonging to some maiden—that sacred room of her own, where she prays her prayers, and lives her most secret life. I have often wondered at the many girls who hang that especial picture over their fire-places. It must be a case of unconscious ideality.

They realize that love must be so subject to honor that heart-strings would break for the sake of that honor, if need be, even though the harmonious love-song of two hearts is hushed; and what is the love-song of any two beings compared to a life-song of honor for the world—those wonderful life-songs that we all know? One of them sings itself so loudly to me now, over ages of romance and history, that I must let my simple story wait and give way to it for a minute.

There was a man who lived once. If God did not create him, Homer did. The Oracle told him that the first man who put foot on the Trojan shores would die. He knew this before he started on his voyage for Greece. He left a wife and home behind him, whom he dearly loved. I wonder if he used to pace the deck of the rich barge, and listen to the men chatting around him, and smile as they planned of returning, proud and victorious, to their homes and their wives.

All the while under his smile he knew he was to die, not in the glory of fight, although his sword swung sharp and bright at his side, not in any thrilling fashion, to be sung of and wept of by his fellows.

All the while the heavy barge sailed on, and at last land came in sight. I wonder if his heart was full when he saw it? Did he remember his wife and his home? Did he feel his life strong within him, and eager as a battle-horse, as he neared the land where wars were to be fought, and glories won?

All the while his heart was firm. He stood the very foremost of them all, as they drifted quite in to the green, green shore. Around him men talked and laughed, and the sun shone. He may have laid his hand commandingly on some youthful shoulders and pushed back the eager boy who longed to bound first into this new world. He may have saved him thus from death for life. We do not know.

All we do know is, that with his own brave feet he marched ahead of them all, solemnly, smilingly, with the oracle in his heart. From the vessel to the green, green shore—such a little step. He leaps from the Grecian barge to the Trojan land, alive. Does he turn to look at his comrades and off eastwards, beyond homewards, with a great thrill before he falls dead? We do not know.

All we do know is, that *we* thrill now as we

see him leaping to his death, even over this gap of ages, through these shadows of unreality.

We have left Mae flashing scorn at Norman for a long while, a much longer while than she really needed for her flash, for Norman's angry start, violent exclamation, and indignant glance convinced her of her mistake before he answered her.

"I refuse to fight—I—Great—I beg your pardon, Miss Mae, but of course I'll fight. I only hope the fellow isn't such a craven as to let it blow over. However, I strongly suspect policy and his friends will keep him from it. For my part, I would like to break my lance for the poor woman. Any good blow struck for the fair thing, helps old Mother Earth a bit, I suppose."

"That's your idea of life?" queried Eric, rather gravely. "My efforts are all to push Eric Madden on his way a bit."

"And I haven't any idea; I just live," said Mae, "like a black and tan dog. I wish I were one. Then the only disagreeable part of me, my conscience, would be out of the way. But what has all this to do with the duel?" "That has something to do with it, I fancy," said Eric, rising and leaving the room hastily, as the bell rang. "No, stay where you are. I'll receive him in the little salon." Mae rose and walked to the fireside, and looked down on the two small logs of wet wood that sizzled on the fire-dogs. The faint, red flame that flickered around them, looked sullen and revengeful, she thought, as she watched the feeble blaze intently. It seemed hours since Eric had left the room. What was Norman thinking? What was the stranger saying out in the little salon? No, no, she would not think thus. She would repeat something to quiet herself — poetry — what should it be? Ah, here is Eric.

It was Eric. His face was flushed. His lip curled. "Coward! craven!" he exclaimed, "Coward, craven."

"Well, tell us about it," said Norman, coolly, but a wave of color rushed over his face.

"O, palaver and stuff. Somebody's dreadfully ill — dying, I believe, and that somebody is wife, or mother, or son to this brute you challenged. He's got to go, the coward. If you are ever in his vicinity again, and send him your card, he will understand it and meet you at such place and with such weapons as you prefer. Bah — too thin!" and Eric concluded with this emphatic statement.

Mae leaned her head against her two clasped hands which rested on the mantel-piece. How strangely everything looked; even the dim fire had a sort of aureole about it, as her eyes rested there again; but when one looks through tears, all things are haloed mistily. Norman turned and looked at Mae, as Eric walked impatiently about. She did not move or speak. He walked to her side, and stood looking down at her. The faint mist in her left eye was forming into a bright, clear globe as large as any April rain-drop. Mae knew this, and knew it would fall, unless she put up her hand and brushed it away, and that would be worse. The color rose to her cheeks as she waited the dreadful moment. She was perfectly still, her hands clasped before her, her head bent, as the crystal drop gathered all the mist and halo in its full, round embrace, and pattered down upon the third finger of her left hand — her wedding-ring finger — and lay there, clear and sparkling as a diamond!

Norman Mann stooped and laid his hand over it. "You are glad, then!" "I should be sorry to have you die," said Mae, but her dimples and blushes and drooping eye-lids said, oh, a great deal more. "Good night," she fluttered, and ran off.

CHAPTER X.

MAE dreamed happy dreams that night, and awoke with a smile on her lips. She dressed with the greatest care, put a touch of the color Norman liked at her throat, and fastened a charm he had given her to her bracelet. Still, she loitered on her way to the breakfast-room, and when she seated herself at the table, a sudden embarrassment made her keep her eyes on her plate, or talk to Eric, or Edith, or any one but Norman. Yet she was perfectly conscious of his every word and motion. She knew he only took two cups of coffee instead of three, and that he helped her to mandarins—a fruit of which she was very fond—five times, so that she had a plate heaping with golden untouched balls before her. After breakfast, she felt a great desire to run away, so she asked Eric to take her to the Capitol, and leave her there for a time. "I want to see something solid this morning, that has lasted a long while, and the marbles will do me good."

Yes, Eric would take her at once. Would she go and get her hat? She went for it, and scolded herself all the time for running away when she wanted to stay home. Yet, after all, who dares put out one's hand to grasp the moon when at last it approaches? No woman, at any rate.

There was a malicious sort of teasing pleasure in running away from Norman, mingled with a shrinking modesty; and, besides, he knew the way to the Capitol, if he chose to follow, and knew she was to be there alone. So, on the whole, Mae went off with a blissful heart.

As she sat down in that celebrated room, immortalized by the Gladiator, the Faun and the Antinous, scales seemed to fall from her eyes and a weight from her heart. Life meant something more than the mere play she delighted in, or the labor she despised. She took it in in this way. She realized, first of all, the enduringness of the marbles. They had stood, they will stand, for thousands of years. What have stood? What will stand? Idle blocks of stone, without form or meaning, or simply three beautiful shapes? No; three souls, thinks Mae, three real people, and she looks at the abiding faun, freedom and joy of the Satyr, the continual sentimental sadness of the Antinous, and the perpetual brave death-struggle of the Gladiator. They are living on now, and touching our hearts. Their mute lips open other eloquent mouths to speak for them. Hawthorne and Byron tell us what the Faun's soul, what the Gladiator's soul, look from the white marbles to us, and the world daily repeats the story the Antinous whispers in his bent, beautiful head, the *vanitas vanitatum* that our own hearts whisper, when we drop earnest life for voluptuous pleasures.

The Faun may smile, although life is only one long play-day in green fields and woods, because he is a Faun. The man must sigh, when he has drained his wine-cups and laughed his heartiest laugh, and wakes to another morning, because he is a man. The cry of humanity echoes in our souls. We cannot stifle it; we may hush it, and follow our idle joys, but the day comes when we bend our head with Antinous and Solomon and the rest of them, and sigh out our *vanitas, vanitas* also, in the great weary chorus.

No need, alas! for a Hawthorne, or Byron, or even a Shakspeare to interpret what the Antinous says for us. Our own hearts do it.

Mae caught the spirit of all this, as her eyes roamed out of the window on the Sabine hills, where woods and springs sang. She saw the aqueducts bounding, even in their ruin, arch after arch, to the treasure house of the waters. "They never can reach it, now," thinks she, "never. Suppose they cannot, is not the spirit the same?" And now Mae is ready for the sudden light that dawns on her soul. She springs to her feet. She is alone in the room with the marble men; and they are quiet; even the Gladiator bites back his last groan once more.

"The Eternal City," shouts Mae; "I know what it means at last. Oh! Rome, Rome, I love you!" and she rests her hand on the window-sill, and looks out on Rome. "Why, it is like a resurrection morn. Ruins? Yes, it is all ruins, dry bones, and great dead in dust; but there is something more. I only saw that graveyard part of it before; now, the spirit of the great men, and great deeds, and words, and thoughts, and prayers," cries Mae, exultantly. "Why, they are here; not dead, like the rest, but alive, all around us. Oh! Rome, Rome, forgive me!"

Now, this might have seemed absurd to the custode, or some other people, if they had put their head in at the door just then. But they didn't; and, really, it was not absurd. I cannot believe that this small Mae Madden is the only being who has had a swift, brilliant awakening from the first surface, depressing thoughts of Rome—an awakening to the living spirits which float proudly over their vacant shells that lie below the old pavements. Once you do feel the strong, rich Roman life about you, the decay, the ruin float off on the dust of the ages, before the glorified breath of proud matrons and stately warriors, who step over the centuries to walk by your side. And the centuries have improved them,—have left their grandeur, and nobility, and bravery, and civilized them a bit. They form into pageants for you, and fill the baths and the palaces, but never crowd the Coliseum for the dreadful contests, unless, maybe, for an occasional bull-fight—some great, horrid, big bull which would be killed at market to-morrow at any rate—and even that is as you please. It is wonderful, truly, once we discern the spirits around us, to notice what a miraculous place Rome is; how the intervening years of purgatorial flames have turned old Nero himself into a fairly benevolent, soft old gentleman, even though his estates have crumbled to such an extent that he may put his golden palace into the head of his cane, which he always carries now, since his chariots have gone away. Where are they? Caligula has even made it up with his mother-in-law, and you reflect with joy on that fact, as the two flit by your mind's eye, hand in hand. All this nonsense is for those of us who *have* awakenings. The rest of "our party" may sit at Spillman's and eat coffee-cakes and sip Lachrymæ Christi, while we walk alone through the Coliseum, with the crowd of old heathen. They stop, every one, at the iron cross in the middle, reared over their carnage and mad mirth, and press their lips to it now. The centuries have done that. We only, alas! stand gazing mournfully, doubtingly. "Will you have another coffee-cake?" says some one, and we remember that we are at Spillman's also. And, indeed, we might be more sensible to stay with our party always; eat cakes, drink wine, laugh at the old world, vaunt the new, read Baedeker and the Bible, say our orthodox Protestant prayers, with a special "Lead us not into Romanism" codicil, and go to bed, and dream of our own golden houses, Paris dresses, and fat letters of credit.

At any rate, Mae Madden was electrified by a great sudden sweep of love, a surging rush of reverence for Rome, and makes no doubt in her own mind, to this day, that the Faun laughed with her in her joy. In this exalted frame of mind, she wandered down through the long halls. She was passing from the room of the Cæsars when she heard Norman's voice. So he had come for her with Eric. She had half fancied he would. She paused to listen. It was a ringing elastic voice, in no wise lagging in speech, with a certain measurement in its tones, as if he weighed his words and thoughts, and gave them out generously, pound for pound, a fair measure which our grandmother's recipes approved. Mae smiled to herself. "He has loved Rome always. He caught the spirit of it long ago. He will be glad to know I have found it also. I wish"—and Mae sighed a scrap of a sigh, and looked down at the toe of her boot, with which she drew little semi-circles before her.

Mae was truly in a very tender mood to-day. I think if Norman had caught sight of her face at that moment, he would have sent Eric off, and right there and then, before all the Cæsars—why what is the matter? The face contracts as if in pain. What was the cause? She had heard Norman say, "I'm afraid I was wrong, but I never meant anything by my attentions to the girl, Eric. It was really on your account. I never liked Miss Rae particularly. I was thrown much with her because you and I have been together constantly, but she does not grow on me. I never expected you should consider me as her necessary cavalier always. As for this evening, I am engaged to Miss Mae, so that settles this matter, but I wish that hereafter you would not get me into such scrapes."

Poor Mae! she leaned against Nero—or was it Caracalla?—surely somebody very hard and cold and cruel,—and stopped breathing for a moment. For she had heard wrong, had misunderstood Miss Rae for Miss Mae, and supposed it was of herself that he spoke. Her heart stood still for the minutest part of a minute. Then she turned softly and quickly, went back to the Gladiator's room, left word with the custode for Eric that she wasn't well, and had gone home alone, walked off down the Capitol steps, took a cab and drove away.

At home she had a long, earnest talk with Lisetta, after which Lisetta had a short, brisk talk with the *padrona*. "It means money," she said, "and I can play I did it for the Signorina's safety." Later, Mae wrote a brief, polite note to Norman Mann. She was ill, had gone to bed, and wouldn't be able to go to the Corso with him to-night. She tried to stifle the hot anger and other emotions out of the words, and read and re-read them to assure herself that they were perfectly easy, natural, and polite. At last she tore them up and sent this instead:

MY DEAR MR. MANN:—Such a pity that we are not to have our fun, after all. Yet, perhaps it is just as well. I should be very speedily without my light, and the cry of "*senza moccolo, senza moccolo*," must be very dispiriting. Have a good time right along. Good-bye —good-bye.

Of course, if Mae had not been beside herself with conflicting emotions, she would never have sent this note, or repeated the good-bye in that echoing, departing sort of way. Norman Mann knit his brow as he read it. "What is the row now?" he thought. "What a child it is, anyway. She has had the mocoletti fun in her mind since we left America, and now she throws it away. Well, there's no help for it; I'm booked for Miss Rae. I'll get Eric to see if Mae's really ill. I wonder if she's afraid of me, because she cried last night, afraid I took that big tear for more than it was worth.

"Mae," said Eric, entering her room an hour later, "Norman feels dreadfully that you are not able to go to-night, and so do I. I suppose those wretched marbles did it this morning. Couldn't you possibly come?"

"No," replied Mae, rising on her elbow, "but sit down a moment, Eric."

"How pretty you look," said her brother, seating himself by her side. Mae's hair was tumbled in brown waves that looked as if they couldn't quite make up their minds to curl, much as they wanted to; her eyes shone strangely; and the little scarlet shawl that she had drawn over her head and shoulders was no brighter than her flushed cheeks. She smiled at her brother, but said hurriedly: "Tell me of your plans for to-night. I suppose you and Mr. Mann are going with your new friends."

"Yes, Norman will go with me and the girls, but he does it with a bad enough grace. He's dreadfully tired of Miss Rae; and, to tell you the truth, Mae, she is rather namby-pamby—very different from Miss Hopkins, and then, besides, he had so set his heart on going with you to-night."

"O, yes," said Mae, scornfully, and bit her lips.

"Why, Mae, what is the matter with you? You seem to doubt every one and everything. You know Norman is truth itself." "Is he?" asked Mae, indifferently.

"I've seen for a long time," continued Eric,

"that you two were not the friends you once were, but I don't understand this open dislike. Doesn't it spoil your pleasure? You don't seem to have the real old-fashioned good times, my little girl," and Eric pulled his clumsy dear hand through a twist of the brown hair caressingly.

"O, Eric," cried Mae, "that is like old times again," and a tear splattered down into the big hand. "What, crying, Mae?" "No, dear — that is, yes. I believe I am a little bit homesick. I wish I could go back behind my teens again. Do you remember the summer that I was twelve — that summer up by the lake? I wish you and I could paddle around in one of the old flat-bottomed tubs once more, don't you, Eric? We'd go for lilies and fish for minnows — that is, we'd fish for perch and catch the minnows — and talk about when you should go to college and pull in the race, and I should wear a long dress and learn all the college tunes to sing with you and your Yale friends. Do you remember, Eric? And now, O dear me, you lost your race, and I hate my long gowns. O — my — dear — brother — do you like it all as well as you thought you would?"

"Why, Mae, you poor little tot, you're sentimental—for you. Yes, I like the future as well as I always did. I never gave much for the present, at any rate."

"But I did, Eric; I always did, till just now, and now I hate it, and I'm afraid of the future, and I'd like to grow backwards, and instead, in a month, I'll have another birth-day, and go into those dreadful twenties." Then Mae was quiet a moment. "Eric, I was sentimental," she said, after a pause. "Really, I do like the future very much. I quite forgot how much for the moment."

"You're a strange child, indeed," replied Eric, the puzzled. "Your words are like lightning. I had just got melted down and ready to reply to your reminiscences by lots of others, and here you are all jolly and matter-of-fact again. I was growing so dreadfully unselfish that I should have insisted on staying home with you this evening to cheer you up a bit."

"And give up the mocoletti! Why, Eric! I shouldn't have known how to take such an offer. No, no, trot off and array yourself, and you may come back and say good-bye."

"I must say good-bye now, dear, for I dine at the Costanzi with the girls and their aunt."

"Now, just now, Eric?"

"Why yes, Mae. You are getting blue again, aren't you? Getting ready for Ash Wednesday to-morrow?"

"Oh, no, no, dear. Kiss me, Eric, again. You're a good, dear boy. No; I didn't cry that drop at all. Good-bye; and to-morrow is Ash Wednesday. But we don't sorrow or fast in Paradise, I suppose."

CHAPTER XI.

THE Corso was all ablaze. The whole world was there. Under a balcony stood a party of peasants. Of this group, two were somewhat aside. One of these was tall, dark, a fair type of Southern Italian; the other small, agile and graceful, dressed in a fresh contadina costume, with her brown hair braided down her shoulders. She seemed excited, and as the crowd pressed nearer she would draw back half-fearfully. "Lisetta," she whispered, "I am spoiling your good time. Talk to your friends; never mind me. I will follow by your side, and soon I shall catch the spirit of it all, too." Saying this, she stepped from under the balcony, held out her feeble little taper and joined in the cries around her, pausing to blow at any lowered bit of wax that came in her way. It was maddening sport; her light was extinguished again and again, but she would plead to have it relit, and there was sure to be some tender-hearted, kindly knight at hand to help her.

She ran on quickly, fearlessly, gliding and

creeping and sliding through the crowd, her hair flying, her eyes dancing. Even in the dense throng many turned to look at her, and one tall man started suddenly from the shadow of a side street, where he had been standing motionless, and threw himself before the girl. He put out his arm, grasped her tightly, and drew her a few feet into the shadow. "Signorina!" he said. "Hush, hush," she whispered then in colder tones. "Let me go, Signor; you are mistaken. You do not know me." He smiled quietly, holding her hands clasped in his. "I do not know you, Signorina? You do not know me. Your face is the picture always before my eyes."

"Yes, yes, forgive me," she fluttered, "I was startled, and indeed I am no Signorina now, but one of your own country peasants. I am with Lisetta. Why, where is Lisetta?"

Where, indeed, was she? There were hundreds of contadine in the great crowd surging by, but no Lisetta. The little peasant wrung her hands quite free from the man's grasp. "I must go home," she said. "I don't want any more Carnival."

"No, no," said the officer, quietly, reassuringly. "Get cool. Tell me how Lisetta looks and is dressed, and if we can not find her here, I will take you up to your friend's balcony."

"O, no, not there. Anywhere else, but not there."

"Why not?" asked Bero.

"Because, because,—yes, I will tell you," said Mae, remembering her wrongs, and suddenly moved by the sympathy and softness of the great eyes above her,—"because they think I am home ill, and here I am, you see," and she laughed a little hurriedly,—"besides, I go away with Lisetta to-morrow morning,—hush, let no one hear,—to Sorrento. You must never, never tell. How do I look? Will I make a good peasant, when once the dear sun has browned my hands and forehead, and I have grown Italianized?" And she lifted her face, into which the saucy gaiety had returned, up to him temptingly.

His warm blood was kindled. "You are a little child of the sun-god now," he exclaimed, passionately. "May I share some of your days in heaven? I am ordered to Naples to-morrow night; shall be only twelve hours behind you. May I come on the day after to see you in your new home?"

"O, how delightful! But, perhaps, my lord, our little cottage by the sea isn't grand enough for your spurs and buttons and glory. We are simple folks you know,—peasants all,—but our hearts, Signor, they are hospitable, and such as we have we will gladly give you. What do you say to the bay of Naples, and oranges for our luncheon day after to-morrow?" And Mae laughed lightly and joyously. Her little burnt taper fell to the ground, and she clasped her hands together. "What a happy thing life will be!"

"Will you live there and be a peasant forever?" asked Bero, leaning forward. "There are villas by the sea, too, Signorina."

Mae didn't hear these last words. Her heart had stood still on that "forever." Live there forever, forever, and never see her mother or Eric, or,—or any one again! "I hadn't thought of that," she said, "I hadn't thought of that." She stood still with her hands clasped, thinking. The officer at her side, looking down at her, was thinking also. He was fighting a slight mental struggle, a sort of combat he was quite unused to. Should he let the child go on in this wild freak? He knew the cottage by the sea; the peasant home would be dreadful to her. He knew that by that same day after to-morrow, life in lower Italy, with the dirty, coarse people about her would be a burden. Yet he hesitated. He fought the battle in this way: Should he not stand a better chance if he let her go? He had his leave of absence for three weeks (this was true; "ordered to Naples," he had called it to Mae). Three weeks away from his world, near this winsome, strange, magnetic little being, with the bay of Naples, and moonlight, and his own glories and her loveliness! He couldn't give up this chance. No, no. He would surely see her in a few hours after her troubles began, and comfort her. So he only smiled quietly down at her again, as she stood troubled by his side, and said: "Lisetta will seek you near your balcony if she knows where it is. Don't be troubled."

"But where is my balcony?" asked Mae.

"Come here," said Bero, leading her slightly forward. She looked up and saw the quiet side-window, where day after day the officer had flung her the sweet flowers when no one was looking. "I know this place very well," he said meaningly. Mae smiled a little cheerfully. "You have beautiful taste," she replied, "I have never seen such exquisite bouquets before."

Bero stroked his moustaches complacently. "You honor me, Signorina. I hope you may receive many, many more beautiful flowers — from the same hand." He whispered these last words, and Mae turned her head half uneasily. She looked up at the balcony. How odd it was that there, but a few feet away, were Mrs. Jerrold, Edith, and Albert. She fancied she could detect their voices, though she could not see them. The Hopkins-Rae window was vacated. "The girls" were probably down on the Corso with Eric and Norman, and Mae drew a little nearer to Bero, and looked up half appealingly. His eyes were fixed strangely on something or some one across the street. Mae followed their gaze, and saw upon the opposite balcony the beautiful veiled lady. She held in her hand a long rod tipped with a blazing taper.

"O, she is like a vestal virgin with her light, or a queen with a sceptre," cried Mae exultingly.

"She may be the vestal virgin, but the queen is by my side," said Bero earnestly.

Mae wished he would not talk in this way, and she tried to laugh it off. "I have no sceptre or crown; I'm but a poor queen in my common garb."

"We'll have the coronation day after to-morrow," replied Bero, very earnestly still.

"Tell me about her," and Mae nodded her

head toward the strange lady. "There is little to tell," said Bero, in a quiet tone. "Her brother is well known in Rome as an artist. He lives there with his sister and an old duenna. She wears this mysterious veil constantly, and some fanciful people see just as mysterious a cloud resting about her life. I only know she is strange and beautiful, and that her name is Lillia."

Yet Bero had seen this woman almost daily for six months. But he only knew she was strange and beautiful, and that her name was Lillia.

Mae had never spoken to the veiled stranger, yet if Bero had turned upon her and asked, "Who is she?" she would have replied: "I do not know her name or where she lives, but I know she struggles, and despairs, and smiles over all. And I know her suffering comes from sorrow—not from sin." But Mae did not say all this. She only looked at the veiled lady. Her vestal lamp had dropped for the moment, and she seemed to be gazing far away. A fold of her heavy veil fell over her brow quite down to her great dark eyes. They were unshaded, yet they too, seemed clouded for the moment. "Her name is Lillia," said Mae, reassuringly to herself. "Her name is Lillia. I am sure she is like her name." Bero smiled. Just then Lisetta appeared.

CHAPTER XII.

EARLY the next morning, in the misty light, Lisetta and Mae, the latter still in her contadina costume, left the house quietly. In an hour the train for Naples was to start, but Lisetta wanted to say her prayers in Rome on this Ash Wednesday. They wandered into a little church, one of the many Roman churches, and knelt side by side, Lisetta with her beads and her penance, and Mae with her thoughts, which grew dreary enough before the peasant was ready to go. Mae had already entrusted her money to Lisetta's keeping—some one hundred and fifty dollars, which she had gotten the day before from Albert to buy clothes with—and with her money she had also resigned all care. She did not know therefore, until the train started, that their seats were in a third-class carriage. Every one was hurrying on board, so Mae was obliged to jump in without a word, and accept her fate as best she could. It was no very pleasant fate. The van was dirty, crowded, garlic-scented. Mae was plucky, however, and knew she was to find dirt and dreadful odors everywhere. Two months of Rome had taught her that. But it grew very dreadful in the close travelling-carriage. There was an old woman at her side, with a deformed hand, and two soldiers opposite, who stared rudely at her, and made loud, unpleasant remarks; and having no books, and nothing to entertain herself with, she was forced to curl up in a corner, and try to sleep, which she could not do.

Poor child! it was a hard day. Dull and dreary outside, and within, the sickening odors and people. Back in Rome, what were they doing? Had they found out that she had gone? And Eric, how was he feeling? No, no, she must not think of all this. It belonged to the past. Before her lay Sorrento, the bay of Naples, oranges, white clouds, and the children of the sun. Mamma was south, too — if she were only going to her. So the day dragged on, until with the evening they reached Naples. They spent the night with a friend of Lisetta, who rented apartments to English and Americans. Mae was fortunate, therefore, in securing an unlet bedroom that was comfortably furnished. She enjoyed listening to Lisetta's stories of Rome and the Carnival; and after a quiet night in a clean bed, awoke tolerably happy and very eager for her first sight of the bay. They took an early train out to Castellamare, and as they left the city, Mae wondered if Bero were just entering it. But she soon forgot him and every one in the blue glories of the bay.

At Castellamare, Gaetano, Lisetta's husband, was awaiting them, with a malicious little donkey, tricked out gaily enough in tags of color and tinkling bells. It was very quaint and delightful to get into the funny, low, rattling cart, and go jogging off, while the feminine sight-seers fanned themselves in the windows of the ladies' waiting-room, and grumbled, and the poor masculine travellers bartered in poor Italian, with their certain-to-conquer enemies, those triumphant swindlers, the drivers of the conveyances between Sorrento and Castellamare

Then they began that wonderful ride along the coast. The horrors of the day before rolled away like a mist as the donkey jogged along that miraculous drive. Lisetta and Gaetano chattered together, and Mae sat very still, with her face to the sea, drinking in all the glory, as she had longed and planned. Hope revived in her breast, pride had stood by her all the while, and here was glorious nature coming to her aid. She was going swiftly to the orange groves and the children of the sun. She should see Talila and brown babies and dancing, and at night a great, yellow moon would light up the whole scene. So on and on they went, the travelling carriages dashing by them now and then, with their three donkeys abreast, and the driver cracking his whip, and the travellers oh-ing and ah-ing.

"That is the most picturesque peasant I have yet seen," said a gentle lady in brown to her husband, as they passed the humble little party. "Yes, she is clean, and more like the ideal than the actual peasant, and I am very glad I have seen her."

Really, Mae was for the moment, at a quick glance, the ideal peasant. Her hands lay in her lap, her face was toward the sea, and her attitude and features were all full of that glow of existence that peasant portraits possess. She lived and moved and had her being as part of a great, warm, live picture. If the lady in brown had not passed so quickly, however, she would have seen a something in Mae's face that spoiled her for a peasant, an earnestness in her admiration, a sharp intensity in her joy, that was very different from the languid content of a Southern Italian. Her movements were rather like those of the Northern squirrel, which climbs nimbly and frisks briskly, than like the sinuous, serpentine motions of the Southern creatures of the soil. We are, after all, born where we belong, as a rule, and the rest of us soon belong where we are born.

After a time the donkey pattered along towards a little patch of houses on the shore. They had already passed a half dozen of similar settlements. Very dirty children ran about crying, ugly old women knitted, mongrel dogs and cats barked and yelped and rolled in the mud. Bits of orange-peel and old cabbage and other refuse food lay piled near the doors. There were, to be sure, young girls with dark eyes, plaiting straw, and the very dirt heaps had a picturesque sort of air. An artist might linger a moment to look, but never to enter. Yet it was here that Mae must enter. This was her new home. The neighbors came crowding about curiously, and she was hurried into the little hut that seemed as if it were carved roughly from some big garlic, probably by taking out the heart of it for dinner. Mae hardly comprehended the situation at first, but when she began to realize that this was a substitute for sea breeze, and that the coarse clipped patois (which sounded worse in the mass than when it fell from Lisetta's lips alone) was in place of the flowing melody of speech she had longed for, she grew sick at heart. The folly, the dreadfulness of what she had done, swept over her like a flood, and with it came dreadful fear. She was helpless,—an outcast. Pride would never let her go home. She could go nowhere else. They had her money, and here she must live and die. She sat down in a sort of stupor, and paid no heed to the squabbling children who pulled at her gown, or the dogs who sniffed snappingly at the stranger.

Lisetta, busy with greetings and chattings, quite forgot her for a time, and was dismayed when she saw her sitting disconsolately by. "Come, Signorina," she cried, "go down to the bay. Here is Talila; she will guide you."

Mae looked up quickly at that. Talila, was she here? A few feet from her she saw an uncouth woman, with that falling of the jaw most imbeciles possess, and a vacancy in her eyes. She had her hand raised and was swearing at one of the children. "Talila," repeated Mae, rubbing her eyes, and shivering, "but I thought Talila would be different. You said she loved children, but this woman swears at them."

"O, dear, we all swear at them, but we love them; you shall see how they follow her. Talila, off with you and your babies." And the next moment there was a general scamper of brown children headed by this tall, vacant-looking woman. "Take the lady to the sea," continued Lisetta. And Mae arose, as if in a dream, and followed them.

The half-clad children of the sun ran before her as she had dreamed they would; flowers sprang up along the way, but she did not stop to pluck a single bud or turn to look at anything. She wandered on in an awful sort of fright and came at length to the water's edge. Here there were row-boats lying at anchor, into which the children clambered. Mae stepped into one of them and sat down in the stern, and looked about. All was as she had planned. Her day of heaven was here. She tried to be brave. O, she tried very hard. She wanted to love and enjoy the sea, and think beautiful thoughts. She roused a little and stretched herself out to catch the sunbeams in her eyes, as she had said she would. How warm they were. An umbrella would be a luxury—and a book! But these belonged to the world she had left so far behind her. The dirty children babbled a strange tongue; the water around the boat, by the shore, was covered with a scum, and alas! alas! the land of her desire was farther off than ever. Then she remembered that Norman Mann had once said: "If you ever do disappear I shall know where to look for you." Would he think of it now? Would he come for her? If he had only come last night, and would drive by now to Sorrento. He would be here soon if he had. Would she call him loudly or shrink down in the boat and hide her face in her hands till she knew he was a long way past? The rest of them would not know where to look for her. They did not know anything about Lisetta, and she had promised not to tell even the *padrona.* (Faithless Lisetta!) But of course Norman wouldn't come for her, after what he had said at the Capitol. That was what finally drove her away. How unlike him it did seem to speak of her in that way to Eric. She thought over his words, and as she did so she seemed to see her mistake, and grasp his meaning.

She sprang up in the boat. "It was the other

girl — Miss Rae — he was speaking of. Oh, oh, oh — and now it is too late. He will hate me always."

As she stood there, a carriage rolled by. Some one looked out. "O, mamma," said a young voice in English, "look at that pretty little peasant," and a kid-gloved hand was stretched through the open window to spatter a shower of base coin toward her. It was terrible! The children sprang for it, and, fighting and laughing, ran homewards with the dreadful Talila. The parti-colored picturesque dress had been a joy to Mae. Now she longed to tear it off and die — die! No, she was afraid to die. She would have to live, and she didn't know how, and she laughed a bitter sort of laugh.

There was a sound of horses' feet again. The road lay almost close to the shore just here. A low exclamation, a vault from his horse, which was speedily cared for by a dozen boys near at hand, and before Mae knew it, the officer was beside her once more.

O, how beautiful it was to see some one from the world, fresh, and clean, and fair. Mae gazed at him in delight, and sprang up warmly, holding out both her hot hands. "How is

Heaven?" asked Bero, as he raised the white fingers to his lips.

"That is not the custom with us," said Mae, withdrawing her hand.

"But what is custom in Heaven?" he laughed. "Can't we do as we please in our Heaven, Signorina?"

"This isn't our Heaven, and I don't please. O, how could you let me come to this dreadful place. Did you know how awful it would be?"

"Shall I tell you why I said nothing? Let me row you away from all this," and he began to untie the boat.

"When did you come?" asked Mae.

"I left Rome last night, reached Naples this morning, and here I am as soon as possible, Signorina."

Mae felt herself gradually yielding to the spell of this man's soft power. She had grown strangely quiet and passive, and she folded her hands and looked off seawards in a not unhappy way. She seemed to be some one else in a strange dream.

"Are you glad I came?" asked Bero, as he jumped into the boat and sat down opposite her. Mae did not reply. She had almost lost the power of speech. She only smiled feebly and faintly. Bero had never seen her thus before, but he realized dimly that it was he who had changed her, and the sense of his own power excited him the more. He bent his proud head and flashed his beautiful eyes as he lifted the oars to the locks, and silently pulled out toward the bay.

As he rowed he gazed fixedly at her, and the frightened, puzzled child could not turn her eyes from his. His look grew softer and tenderer, his head bent towards her, the oars moved slower and slower and at last stopped imperceptibly. Still the man gazed passionately, claimingly, and the girl breathed harder and let her eyes rest on his, as if he had been a wondrous, charming serpent, and she a little, unresisting dove. Then he spoke.

His words were so low, it seemed as if his eyes had found voice; his words were so caressing, it seemed as if they changed to kisses as they fell. "Listen," he said, softly, and drew up his dripping oars and let the boat drift—"Listen. This is not our Heaven, but I know a villa by the sea. There are hills and woods about it; flowers, fruits, and in the day, sunshine, at night, moonlight and music; drives, and walks, and vines, and arbors. Could you find there your Heaven—with me? May I take you to my villa?"

When he ceased, his words dropped slowly into silence, and Mae still gazed at him. She saw him come nearer to her, with his eyes fixed on hers; she saw his hand leave the oar and move slowly toward hers, but she was motionless, looking at the picture he had painted her of life — the cloudless days, moonlit nights — the villa by the sea — the glowing Piedmontese. Her eyelids trembled, her pulse beat.

Could she take that villa for her home? That man for her husband? She had half thought till now in soft luxurious Italian, but 'my home' and 'my husband' said themselves to her in her own mother tongue. She gave a long shiver, and pulled her eyes from his. It was like waking from a dream. "No — oh, no; take me home," she gasped, and turned toward the shore, where, erect, with folded arms and head bared, stood Norman Mann.

The Italian bit his lip, and said something under his breath, but he took the oars and pulled ashore. Mae turned her eyes downward and felt the color creep up, up into her cheeks. It seemed eternity. The boat was Charon's, and she was drifting to her fate. Norman Mann stood like a statue. The wind moved his hair over his forehead, and once Mae saw him toss the unruly locks back in a familiar way he had. She did not know why, but the tears half came to her eyes as he did it. He stood as firm and hard and still as a New England rock, while the Italian swayed lithely as he pulled the oars, with the curve and motion of a sliding, slippery stream.

The boat came safely ashore. The Piedmontese helped her to land, and the three stood silent; but Mae under all her shame felt content to be near Norman. His voice broke the quiet, quick and clear. "Are you married?" he asked.

"I! married! What do you—what can he mean?"

"Why is this man here, then?"

Mae stood an instant so still that the heavy breaths of the two men were distinctly audible, the passionate boundings of Bero's pulse, the long, deep throbs of Norman's heart. The officer stepped toward her. Norman stood unmoved. The Italian's eye wandered restlessly, his hand fell to his sword. Norman's arms were folded, and his face set.

Mae looked at one, then at the other, perplexedly. Then she understood. Like lightning, a terrible temptation flashed into her mind. The

Italian loved her, would shield, protect, honor her. Norman must hate her, would always despise her. Should she lift her little weak woman's hand and place it in the man's hand ready to claim it, or stand still and be crushed by that other hand there?

Ah! she could not do it. She tried once. She held out weakly her right hand toward Bero; but the left stretched itself involuntarily to Norman. Then the two met in each other's pitiful clasp over her bent head, and with a low wailing cry she fell in a little heap on the sand.

When she opened her eyes, they were both bending over her. "Take me home," she gasped to Norman. He glared at the officer. "Go!" he said. Bero put his hand to his sword. Mae sprang up. "No," she said, gently, "no, my friend, for you have always been kind and friendly to me. Pray go." Bero was touched by this. This little girl had taken only good from him, after all, sympathy and friendliness. Norman was touched also with the same thought. Then the officer smiled pleasantly. He shrugged his shoulders slightly, regretfully, and bowed and rode away. And so the clinking spurs and yellow moustaches and amorous eyes vanished from Mae's sight.

As he rode off he was somewhat sorrowful; but he took a picture from his pocket and looked at it. "She'll be glad to welcome me back again," he said to himself, pleasantly, "and she belongs to my own land. This little foreigner might have pined for her own home, by and by." Then he sighed and shook his head. "Alas! this little stranger will dance before you often, still!" and he touched his eyes; "but I will put you back in your place here, now." This he said, looking at Lillia's picture and with his hand on his heart.

CHAPTER XIII.

"TAKE me home," said Mae again imploringly. "Not back there," as Norman drew her hand through his arm and started for the hut, "O no, not even for a minute."

"Sit here then," he replied quietly, "while I arrange it with the woman," and he walked quickly away. Mae watched him till he entered the low doorway, in a sort of subdued, glorified happiness, that would break out over her shame and fear. She was afraid he would hate her, at least she told herself so, but in reality, everything and everybody and every place were fast fading out of this eager little mind. She and Norman were together, and she could not help being content. There was a certain joy in her weakness and shame, though they were genuine and kept her hushed and silent.

Poor Lisetta was very much frightened, but told her story to this angry stranger with true Southern palaver. She said the little lady loved Italy so, and wanted to be a peasant, and insisted she would run away quite by herself if

Lisetta would not take her, and so she consented, knowing she could, through the *padrona*, send word to the friends.

"And the man?" asked Norman, impatiently.

"What man? O, the officer. He just rode down this morning for a morning call. I never saw him before."

A great weight, as large as the Piedmontese, fell from Norman's heart then, and he scattered money among the children recklessly and ordered up the donkey, and smiled on the amazed Lisetta all in the same breath, and went back to help Mae into the wagon with the lightest kind of a heart. It was a strange ride they took back to Castellamare. I think they both wished the world could stand still once more. When they had arrived at the station they found the next train to Naples was not due for two hours. Norman left Mae in the waiting-room for a time. Through the window she watched Gaetano and the donkey start homeward, with a great sigh of relief. She had time while she was sitting to think, but her head was in too great a whirl. She could only feel sorry and ashamed and meek and happy, all mixed together. The sensation was odd.

"I have telegraphed Eric that we would start

home by the next train, that you had only been off for a frolic. I hope we can buy a waterproof or shawl and a hat in Naples for you?"

"Yes," said Mae, meekly, "I have my waterproof here. I think I will put it on now, please," and she began nervously to untie the shawl strap. Norman put her fingers gently aside, and unbuckled it for her. He handed her the long deep-blue cloak, which she put tightly about her, drawing the hood over her head. "You look like a nun," said Norman, smiling. "I wish I were one," replied Mae, with a choke in her throat. She was growing very penitential and softened.

"What shall we do now?" asked Mr. Mann. "We have a long time to wait. If you feel like walking, we can find a pleasanter spot than this." "Go anywhere you please," replied Mae meekly.

"What is the matter with you?"—for Norman had a very amused expression in his brown eyes.

"I hardly recognize you. Not a trace of fight so far, and it must be two hours since we met.

"Don't," said Mae, with her eyes down, so of course he didn't, but the two just marched quietly along back on the Sorrento road towards some high rocks. They sat down behind these, with their faces towards the sea, and were as thoroughly hidden from view, as if they had been quite alone in the world.

"I suppose they were frightened," asked Mae, "at home—at Rome, I mean." "Dreadfully," replied Norman, trying to be sober, but with the glad ring in his voice still. "Edith was for dragging the Tiber; she was sure you and the seven-branched candlestick lay side by side. Mrs. Jerrold searched your trunks and read all your private papers, I am morally certain." Then Norman stopped abruptly, and Mae drew the long stiletto from her hair nervously and played with it before she said, "And the boys?" "Albert was very, very sad, but reasonably sure you would be found. We all feared the Italian, but Albert worked carefully, and soon discovered that the officer was said to be engaged to a young girl with whom he had been seen the day after you left, and that gave him courage,"—then Norman stopped again abruptly. "And Eric?" "Eric sat down with his face in his hands and cried, Miss Mae, and said, 'I've lost my sister, the very dearest little sister in the world.'"

"And you came and found me," said Mae, after a pause, wiping the tears from her eyes. "Yes, thank God," said Norman. He was sober enough now. "Why did you do it?" asked Mae, "when I had been so naughty, and silly, and unkind?" He came very near telling her the reason as she looked up at him, but he did not, for she dashed on, "O! Mr. Mann, I have been—"

"Don't confess to me, Miss Mae. Leave all of this till you get home to your own, who have a right to your confessions and penitence. Never mind what you have been, here you are, and as I have only one more handkerchief and your own looks as if it had been sea-bathing, you had better dry your eyes and be jolly for the next two hours." This was a precarious speech, but Mae only laughed at it,and dried her eyes quickly. "But I have one thing to say to you," she said, "and please mayn't I?"

"You may say anything you please to me, of course," replied this very magnanimous Norman.

"It is not about the miserable past or my doings, but it's about the future. I've said good-bye to my dreams of life—the floating and waving and singing and dancing life that was like iced champagne. I'd rather have cold water, thank you, sir, for a steady drink, morning, noon and night. I'm going to be good, to read and study and grow restful,"—and Mae folded her hands and looked off toward the sea. "She's a witching child," thought Norman. Then she raised her head. "I said it lightly because I felt it deeply," she added, as if in reply to his thought. "I am going to grow, if I can, unselfish and sympathetic, and perhaps, who knows, wise, and any way good."

"There is no need of giving up your champagne entirely. Give yourself a dinner party now and then o' holidays. The world is full of color and beauty, and poetry you love. All study is full of it — most of all it lives in humanity."

"Well," said Mae, "aren't you glad I'm going to change so?"

"I'm glad you're going to give your soul a chance. Your body has been putting it down hard of late."

"It's but a weakling," said Mae, with a shake of her head, "and I've hardly heard its whimpers at all, but—O, Mr. Mann, if you could have seen Talila—she's dreadful."

"Who is Talila? and what has she to do with your soul?"

"O, she's one of those Sorrento people," replied Mae, as if she had lived there for years. "I have so much to tell you: it will take—"

"Years, I hope, dear." The last word dropped without his noticing it, but Mae caught it and hid it in her heart.

"What made you think of coming for me?" she asked, after a pause, during which Norman had hummed a song as she had been writing her name on the sand. They were quite on the shore and only a narrow stretch of beach separated them from the bay. "You said if you ever came away, you would go to Sorrento, and I knew you had a friend in the kitchen who lived near Naples. So I searched for her and the *padrona*, and, finding neither of them, set Giovanni a babbling, and learned that the woman Lisetta had left that morning for Sorrento. I told the boys I had a mere suspicion that I would trace for them. So off I came last night, and by stopping and enquiring at every settlement, at last discovered you."

"This is my birth-day; I am twenty years old," said Mae. "Why, what are you doing?" For Norman had bent down to the sand also, and had drawn a queer little figure there.

"That is you when you were one year old," he laughed, "and you could only crow and kick your small feet, and smile now and then, and cry the rest of the time."

"That is about all I can do yet," said Mae.

"Here comes number two," and he drew his hand across the sand and smoothed the baby image away, leaving in its place a round, sturdy little creature, poised dangerously on one foot. "You have walked alone, and you have called your father's name, and you're a wonderful child by this time."

"This is the three-year-old, white aprons and curls, please observe. Now, you recite 'Dickery, dickery dock' and 'I want to be an angel,' and you have cut all your wisdom teeth."

"O, Mr. Mann, I haven't cut them yet. Babies don't have them."

"Don't they? Well, you have other teeth in their place, white and sharp—but by this time you are four years old."

"Ah, here I begin to remember. You draw the pictures, and I'll describe myself. Four years old!—let me see—I had a sled for Christmas, and I used to eat green apples. That's all I can remember; and five and six years old were just the same."

"O, no, I'm sure you went to church for the first time somewhere along there; and isn't that a noteworthy event? I suppose all your thoughts were of your button boots and your new parasol?"

"I behaved beautifully, I know; mamma says so; sat up like a lady, while you were sleeping, on that very same Sunday, off in some little country church, I suppose."

"I shouldn't wonder—sleeping in my brother's outgrown coat into the bargain, with the sleeves dangling over my little brown hands."

"It doesn't seem as if they could ever have been very little, does it, Mr. Mann?"

Mr. Mann unfolded five fingers and a thumb and surveyed them gravely for a moment. "It is strange that this once measured three inches by two and couldn't hit out any better than your's could."

Mae had laid her hand on her knee and was looking at it also in the most serious manner. Now she doubled it into a small but very pugnacious looking fist, which she shook most entrancingly before the very eyes of the young man by her side. The eyes turned such a peculiar look upon her that she hastened to add: "Go on with your dissolving views. It is number eight's turn next. You are the showman, and I am interested spectator."

"You insist upon describing my pictures, so I think you are properly first assistant to the grand panorama. Here's eight-year-old. Try your powers on her."

"Let me see. O, then I read all the while, the 'Fairchild Family' and 'Anna Ross,' and I used to wear my hair in very smooth braids, I remember. I was ever so good."

"Impossible; you must have forgotten," suggested Norman. "You surely whispered in school and committed similar dreadful crimes. Poor little prig."

"No, don't," plead Mae; "please don't laugh at the little girl me. I love to think of her as so goody-goody. Last night," and Mae lowered her voice, "I seemed to see little Mae Madden kneeling down in the old nursery in her woolly wrapper saying her prayers," and Mae brought up on the prayers very abruptly, and bent over toward the sand and began to draw hastily. "Here comes nine-year-old Mae. Mr. Mann, you may do the describing."

"O, I suppose there were doll's parties, first valentines, and rides with Albert in his buggy, when you clung very tightly to the slight arm of the carriage and smiled very bravely up in his face. You must have been pretty then."

"No, I was dreadfully ugly. I had broken out two teeth climbing a stone wall."

"You had stopped being good?"

"Yes, that only lasted a little bit of a time."

"Miss Mae, I'm sure you were never ugly, but naughty and silly, I dare say. Kept a diary now, didn't you?"

"Yes, and went to sleep with Eliza Cooke's poems under my pillow every night, and my finger holding the book open at some such thrilling verse as this:

'Say on that I'm over romantic
  In loving the wild and the free,
But the waves of the dashing Atlantic,
  The Alps and the eagle for me.'"

"Did you wear your hair plaited when you were ten years old?" enquired Norman, intensely busy with another drawing.

"O no; I didn't do anything when I was ten years old but get mad and make up with my two dearest friends."

"One of whom was your dearest friend one-half of the time and the other the rest of it, I suppose."

"Don't be satirical, sir. I had a lover when I was eleven; I used to skate with him and write him little notes, folded very queerly."

"Why do you draw twelve and thirteen with their heads down?" asked Mae, after a moment.

"Because they read so much; everything they

can get hold of, including, possibly, a very revised edition of 'Arabian Nights'?"

"Yes," laughed Mae, "and my first novel, 'Villette.'"

"You go to a play for the first time now," suggested Norman. "How you clasp your hands and wink your eyes and bite your lips! And next day, in front of your mother's pier-glass, how you scream 'O, my love,' and gasp and tumble over in a heap in your brown calico, as the grand lady did the night before, in her pink silk."

"Brown calico, indeed! I never condescended to die in my own clothes, let me assure you. The garret was overhauled, and had been since I was a mere baby, for effective, sweeping garments. Let us hurry along over fourteen and fifteen. I was sentimental and tried to be so young-ladyish then. I used to read history with Albert, and always put on both my gloves when I started out, and had great horror of girls who talked loud in the street. I learned to make bread, and shirt bosoms, and such things."

"Well, here you are in a long dress, Miss Sweet Sixteen. I remember you home from boarding school on a vacation."

"What did you think of me?" asked Mae,

"didn't we have a nice time that summer? O, how silly I was!"

She hurried on, because the eyes had given her that peculiar look again, which put her heart in a tremble. "I did have a beautiful time at boarding school," she continued, "the darlingest principal and such girls."

"Then I suppose you wrote a salutatory in forlorn rhyme to end off with," laughed Norman, "and read it, all arrayed in white, in a trembling voice, and everybody applauded, and even old Judge Seymour admired it, while you were reading, with your pink cheeks and trembling hands and quivering voice."

"Abominable! I didn't have the salutatory, and the girl who did, read a superb one, as strong and masculine—"

"Then the Judge went to sleep, I'm sure," declared Norman.

"Well," said Mae, "you are leaving out two years," for Norman had leaned back against the rock with his arms folded.

"By and by," said Norman, "we all come off to Europe, and some of us go through the heart-ache, don't we?"

"Yes," replied Mae, softly.

"But come out ahead one day at Sorrento,

perhaps?" asked Norman. To which Mae made no direct reply.

"All the Mae Maddens have faded away," she said, looking down at the sand again. "The tide is rising." And she walked forward to the ripples of water, and then came slowly back and stood before Norman seriously. He laughed.

"Why, Mr. Mann," said Mae, "I have been so very, very wicked."

The dreadful Mr. Mann only laughed again.

"You act as if it were all a joke. I never saw you so merry before."

"I have never been as happy before in my life."

"Why?" asked Mae, in a low voice.

"Because I have found you," he answered earnestly, and before she knew it Mae was lifted in the strong, manly arms, her pink cheek close to Norman's brown one, and his lips on hers. She leaned her face against his and clung tightly to him.

"O, Mr. Norman Mann," she said, "do you really want me as much—as I do you?"

And Norman, still holding her tightly, bent his hand, with hers clasped in it, to the sand,

and after the Mae Madden, he wrote another name, so that it read:

MAE MADDEN MANN.

Then he said a great many, many things, all beginning with that electric, wonderful little possessive pronoun " my," of which he had discoursed formerly, and he held her close all the while, and they missed the next train for Naples.

The gay peasant costume fell about the girl's round lithe form like the luxuriant skin of some richly marked animal; but out of her eyes looked a woman's tender, loving, earnest soul. Norman Mann had saved her.

CHAPTER XIV.

EDITH was quietly married to Albert at Easter time, in the English Chapel at Florence. The event was hastened by the sudden appearance of Mae's parents, who set sail soon after hearing of the Sorrento escapade and the embryonic engagement, which awaited their sanction before being announced. Everything was beautifully smooth at last. Edith and Albert left the day of their marriage for Munich, and later, Mrs. Jerrold was to settle down with them at Tuebingen. The rest of the party were to summer in Switzerland; then came fall, and then —what?

Norman thought he knew, and Mae said she thought he didn't, but this young woman was losing half her character for willfulness, and Norman was growing into a perfect tyrant, so far as his rights were concerned. Easter is a season of marriages. Mae read in a Roman paper the betrothal announcement of the Signor Bero and Signorina Lillia Taria. "I would like to send them a real beautiful present," said she, and Norman did not say no. So these two hunted all over Florence, and at length, in the studio of a certain not unknown Florentine, they discovered the very gift Mae desired—a picture of a young Italian soldier, bringing home his bride to his own people. There was the aged mother, proud and happy, waiting to bid the dark-eyed girl welcome. "She has a real 'old Nokomis' air," laughed Mae. "I know she would have told her son not to seek 'a stranger whom he knew not.'" The distant olive-colored hillsides, the splashing fountain near at hand, each face, and even the thick strong sunshine seemed to bear a tiny stamp with Italy graven on it. "The name of the picture is exactly right," said Mae. Under the painting were these words: "Italia Our Home."

Norman would hardly have been human if he had not cast a quick glance at her as she stood thoughtfully before the picture. Mae was almost as good as an Italian for involuntary posing. She had made a tableau of herself now, with one hand at her eyes to shade them from the glare of the sun that fell fiercely through the window, her head half on one side, and a bit of drapery, of lace or soft silk, tight around her white throat. She felt Norman's glance, and looked up quickly, and smiled and shook her head: "No, Italy is not my home, although I love it so well. There is a certain wide old doorway not many miles from New York, and the hills around it, and the great river before it, and the people in it, all belong together, too. That's where we belong, Norman, in America, our home," and Mae struck a grand final pose with her hands clasped ecstatically, and her eyes flashing in the true Goddess of Liberty style.

"Yes, I believe we do, Mae; I am almost anxious to get back and begin work in that young, eager country."

"And so am I," said Mae.

Norman laughed. "To think of your coming down to work, you young butterfly."

"It is what we all have to come to, isn't it? —unless we go to that creature that finds some mischief still for idle hands to do. I don't expect to come to stone-cutting or cattle-driving, but I do expect to settle down into a tolerable housewifely little woman, and—"

"And look after me."

"Yes, I suppose so—and myself, and probably a sewing-class and the cook's lame son.

Heigh-ho-hum! What a pity it is, that it is so uninteresting to be good."

"How do you know?"

"Don't be saucy. I do know, perfectly well, that Mae Madden, naughty, idle, and silly, may be, after all, not so stupid; but get me good, industrious and wise, and it will take all of my time when I'm not asleep to keep so. No, there'll be nothing to say about me any more. I'll be as humdrum as —"

"As I am."

"You — why Norman, are you humdrum?"

"Of course I am, dreadfully humdrum. If you and I were in a story-book, you would have ten pages to my one, to keep the reader awake. But then, story-books aren't the end of life. Suppose you, Mae Madden, have been odd, full of variety, ready to twist common occurrences into something startling and romantic, have you been happy? Haven't you been restless and discontented? Now, can't you, grown humdrum and good, be very happy and contented and joyful, even if the sun rises on just about the same Mondays and Tuesdays and Wednesdays, the year round? You will not do for a story-book then, but won't you do better for life? And, after all, a lively murderer is a great deal more sensational than you could ever be."

"Even when I ran away?"

"Yes. Now, you see, I have been humdrum again, and half preached a sermon."

"All right, sir; so long as you take me for a text, you may preach as you want to, and by and by, I dare say, I shall agree with you."

"It would have been a great deal more interesting if you had married that Italian."

"How do you know I could have married that Italian, my lord? He is going to marry a girl as much more beautiful than I am as—as Bero himself is than you—and yet I would rather have you. And now, don't you dare look at me in that way. I'll never say another nice thing to you if you do. This artist will think we are—"

"Lovers, my dear. And aren't we?"

* * * * * *

Ten days later Norman entered with a letter for Mae. "Read it to me," she said, throwing back the blinds and leaning her elbows on the window-cushion.

"It is from Lillia. Would you rather read it yourself?" "O, no." So Norman read what Lillia had written in her pretty broken English:

"MY DEAR MISS MAE:—Thank you of all my heart for your so lovely gift. I have had so little home since long, long ago my mother died, and now I am to have one as the maid in the picture has. We will marry the fifth day of May at five o'clock, and will wish you to be there. Don't forget me.

LILLIA."

"Signor Bero has added a postscript, Mae, which you can translate better than I." And Norman handed her the letter. Mae translated it thus:

"Did you know all that the picture would say to me, Signorina? Receive my thanks for it, too, and believe I shall always live worthy of my Italy, my wife and friends that I see in the picture, and of another friend who lives so far away, whom I shall never see again, if I have such a friend. Think of my beautiful Lillia on our wedding day. We shall be married at St. Andrea's, at vesper time.

BERO."

"And this is the day," said Mae, dropping the note.

"And the very hour, allowing the bride and the sun a few minutes each," added Norman, glancing at the clock.

They gaze quietly out of the window of their lodgings on the Borgo Ognissante, but Mae sees far away beyond the Arno, into the church of St. Andrea,—music, and pomp, and beautiful ceremony, and before the altar, a woman in her bridal robes, with heavily figured lace falling over her black hair and white forehead, and against her soft cheeks and shoulders. Her great brown eyes have thrown away the mist of sadness for a luminous wedding veil of joy, and she is Lillia, and by her side, erect, proud, glorious, with a lingering ray of light falling on his golden head, is her happy husband, Bero. They stand before the altar of St. Andrea's. "God bless you," says Mae aloud. Then her gaze wanders back to the coral and mosaic shops below in the street, and up across to the opposite window, where a long-haired, brown-moustached, brown-eyed man leans, puffing smoke from his curved lips, and holding his cigarette in his slender fingers. She meets his gaze now, as she has met it before. " He is wondering what life will bring to these two young people, I fancy," says Mae.

"Our own wedding-day, Mae," Norman replies; and they both forget all about Lillia, and Bero, and the stranger, and suddenly leave the window. The long-haired man puffs his cigar in a little loneliness, and wishes that wedding bells might ring for his empty heart too.

THE END.

www.ingramcontent.com/pod-product-compliance
Lightning Source LLC
LaVergne TN
LVHW011222110826
845150LV00006B/1510

* 9 7 8 1 4 2 5 5 1 5 6 5 2 *